CULLY: RETRIBUTION

ORRIS SLADE

Contents

Chapter 1

Samuel "Cully" McCullough rode on the back of his loyal horse, Samson. They trudged through the deep snow and waded across half-frozen streams. Steam rose from their bodies as though the heat was trying to escape. Saddlebags jingled and rattled as Samson's hooves beat against the frozen ground. Cully was tired, saddle-raw, and beaten down as the dry winter air burned in his lungs.

It wasn't long before they reached home. Cully couldn't wait to put away the saddle and rest his aching bones beside a warm fire. He would kill for a home-cooked meal and a hot bath. Samson stumbled over a small dip in the ground but righted his gait. Cully patted his horse lovingly.

Shouts echoed through the trees.

Cully placed his hand on the rifle that lay across his lap and listened quietly. He urged Samson into a gallop when the sound of a woman wailing grated against his nerves. They struggled up a steep incline to get a better view of the surrounding area. A young man was hogtied just a few feet away from a nearby gully where about twenty head of cattle were grazing and drinking from the stream.

Three cattle rustlers were too busy roughing up a young lady to notice him on top of the hill. Their laughter caused ice to form in Cully's veins. There wasn't anything he hated more than a man who had the gall to put his hands on a woman.

The cattle rustlers had obviously set out to cause a bit of trouble by robbing these poor folks of their livelihood. Raids were getting worse throughout most of Colorado and Wyoming—even more so for the small ranches and farms just outside of the major settlements. The world was getting bigger, and there wasn't much room left for the little people trying to make an honest living. They either got bought out or robbed blind.

He had seen enough.

Cully raised his rifle to the sky, pulled back on the hammer, and squeezed the trigger of his Winchester. He fired two rounds into the air and cautiously approached the situation. One of the cattle rustlers pulled the woman against him and placed a pistol to her temple.

Cowards... Cully had no patience for cowards.

"What do we got goin' on here, boys?" he asked, slowly dismounting Samson, keeping his rifle level on the man with the gun. The two with the knives weren't going to be much of a problem unless they made a run for the shotguns propped against the felled tree to the left. They were just stupid enough to try it, too. But he would be ready—he always was.

"Why don't you mind your own business?" one of them spat.

Cully assessed the situation. It was obvious that these three fools had intended to entertain themselves with the young lady before they killed the hogtied gentleman and left with the cattle. The unarmed cattle rustlers did exactly what he expected them to do and lunged for the shotguns.

Cully pulled the trigger, lining up his shot with the shorter one's chest. He took the shot.

The rustler went down like a sack of rocks getting tossed into a lake. Blood fanned out around the body as lifeless eyes looked up at him. The woman screamed and began to tremble from head to foot. Cully needed to make quick work of the rustlers so he could focus on keeping her stable until they made it into town.

The other two rustlers started rambling off at the mouth.

"Dang it all to heck! You shot Irwin!" one of them shrieked.

The cattle rustler with the woman began to shiver in his boots. His hands were unstable and shaking as they loosely gripped the pistol.

"If y'all are done cryin' like a bunch of lonely school maids at a social, we can get this confrontation settled." Cully chuckled. "You ain't got a chance of squeezin' off a shot before you end up on the ground like your friend. Not with them hands shakin' the way they are. So why don't y'all just drop your guns and back away slowly?"

"We ain't doin' that!"

"I'll give you one more chance to set down your guns. I'll even let you tell every yellow-bellied vermin you meet behind bars that you walked away from a gunfight with Cully McCullough," he offered, hoping the senseless brutes had heard of him.

From the looks on their faces, he had been correct in his assumption. They dropped their guns and raised their hands.

"Thank you, kindly. Now get on your knees and keep your hands up."

The young woman was in shock, standing less than a foot from the dead body on the ground. Cully walked toward her slowly as though he was calming down a frightened mare. His voice dipped into his lower register as he said, "You'll be all right, now. What's your name?"

"Lenora. My name is Lenora Dunlap, sir."

"Although I wish it had been under better circumstances, it is a pleasure to meet you, Mrs. Dunlap. Is that man tied up over there your husband?"

She looked up at Cully and nodded her head. "We got married in March. His name is Jackson."

"Why don't you go untie your husband so the three of us can have a conversation about how you got into this mess?" Cully waited for Mrs. Dunlap to rush to her husband's side. Giving her a task would help to ease her mind of the trauma of watching a man die. No matter how evil the person, death was death, and people couldn't help grieving.

Cully could tell Mrs. Dunlap was the type of woman who prayed for others more than herself. "How did these three yahoos get the jump on you?"

Once the gag was out of Jackson Dunlap's mouth, he answered the question. "We were having a tough time getting the ranch going after Lenora's father died. There ain't been any money coming in for a while now, so we were headed to the cattle auction to sell these twenty head to get us started."

"And these three saw you as easy pickin'? Not surprised. Y'all should have read the papers. You would have found out about the raids happenin'. Rustlers are comin' from all over the four corners and beyond to get their hands on some good livestock." They had to have been desperate to risk a ride through the harsher territories. Although outlaws were becoming rarer with each day, there were still bad men who wanted nothing more than to watch the world burn.

"Yes, sir. We should have been more careful." Mrs. Dunlap still seemed to be in a bit of shock but grateful, nonetheless.

Cully wasn't about to argue that fact. People needed to be worried about more than just money. Sometimes all a man needed was a comfortable way of life and a clear conscious at the end of the day—which was why Cully had been on his way home.

With no more contracts in the works, he finally had a bit of time to himself to take care of things at the farm.

Mrs. Dunlap finally managed to untie her husband, so Cully instructed them to tie up the bandits with the leftover rope. His rifle was still leveled on the two men as they fixed him with a hateful sneer.

A smile slid across Cully's face. "Y'all be good now, hear. Let these nice folks get you comfortable for the ride out. Puttin' up a fight won't do you much good."

Mrs. Dunlap seemed to be feeling better as she continued to thank Cully for saving their lives. As usual, he had not done it for praise. He saved them because it was the right thing to do, and he had been in the right place at the right time. Doing what was right had always been more important to Cully than gaining recognition. Sure, the reputation he garnered over the years had helped in certain situations. But words of honor, plaques, statuettes, and ribbons made him feel empty inside.

In truth, Cully didn't believe his actions could be lessened to justify a fancy swatch of fabric or a useless bookend he had no intentions of using. It was always the same thing every time: he captured criminals, rode into town, and was greeted by a sheriff, a mayor, or some other stuffed suit that wanted nothing more than a picture with the infamous Cully McCullough to go up on their wall.

No, his good deeds were worth more than that.

After assisting Cully with the cattle rustlers, the Dunlaps continued on to the stockyard in Durango, Colorado.

Cully waved them goodbye and secured the two cattle rustlers on the back of their horses before he carried the dead body over and tied him to his own horse. Just over an hour later, Cully arrived in Durango with three horses trailing behind him. The two rustlers started throwing a fit once they realized he was about to hand them over to the authorities. He may have spared their lives, but he wasn't about to let them go.

He whistled and waved down the sheriff who was nursing a steaming cup of coffee as he walked down the street. The sheriff smiled when he saw Cully, but it quickly faded once he noticed the two men restrained and secured on the back of the horses. He shook his head when he saw the body of the other rustler. "Brought you a few cattle rustlers. You can lock up these two, but the other one made friends with the end of my rifle, as I'm sure you noticed."

"Always keepin' the fun for yourself, Cully."

Cully jumped down from the saddle and followed the sheriff to his office where he gave him a quick rundown on what happened. "Mr. Jackson Dunlap and his lovely wife, Lenora, found themselves the unfortunate victims of these blokes I got strapped to them horses outside."

"It's a good thing you came across them when you did. No tellin' what them poor folks would have gone through if you hadn't," the sheriff said.

He received a small bounty for turning the cattle rustlers over to the authorities, but he handed the money over to Jackson Dunlap, who was standing outside of the sheriff's office to thank him. It wasn't much, but it would help them out with establishing their ranch. He knew what it was like to watch your dreams get crushed beneath the boot of poverty and strife. "Keep yourselves safe. I won't always be there to help out, so you'll have to at least purchase a rifle for when y'all travel through the more dangerous areas in these parts. And put that money toward your ranch."

Jackson Dunlap shook Cully's and the sheriff's hand, accepting the money with honest appreciation in his stare. Mrs. Dunlap turned to Cully with tears glistening in her eyes. "Thank you, Mr. McCullough. We are forever grateful for the kindness you have shown us. Most folks would not have stopped and just ignored my cries for help, but not you. You truly are everything they say about you."

Cully was shocked when Mrs. Dunlap threw her arms around him and embraced him in a tight hug. He didn't know what to do except keep his expression composed and to hold his arms awkwardly at his side until she released him.

Cully cleared his throat and smiled politely in her direction. "It wouldn't have sat right in my gut to leave y'all in distress when I could have prevented it."

"You're my hero, Mr. McCullough. There was no saying what those men would have done to me if you hadn't arrived when you did. I will never forget your bravery and selflessness. We need more people like you in the world."

Mrs. Dunlap burst into tears and pulled Cully in for another awkward hug. Jackson Dunlap thanked him over and over again, shaking Cully's hand to emphasize his sincerity. Cully removed himself from the clutches of Mrs. Dunlap and tipped his hat to her husband.

The only thing left to do was to climb back into the saddle and head on home. Samson neighed as though he could read Cully's thoughts. Both of them were eager to relax and settle their nerves after several close scrapes in the previous months. "Let's go home, Samson."

Chapter 2

Monte Vista, Colorado

The little settlement of Monte Vista was providing housing for the men working on the railroads and those headed for the mines. Drinking among the small crowd of hardworking folks was Louis "Shorty" Gerhard, who ironically stood at six foot five. He was known for his short temper and unbiased selection of who he aimed it toward.

No man, woman, nor child was safe from his wrath.

Shorty had a lucrative business. Stagecoaches and banks helped fund the bigger operations, but the real money was in robbing trains. Having been made notorious by the number of trains he'd successfully robbed over the years, it wasn't hard to find men among the workers who were willing to toss their morals aside and lend a hand for the right price.

But this time, Shorty needed to be careful about whom he trusted. There was a thousand-dollar bounty on his head, and plenty of people were looking to cash in on the reward. Although the six men he rode into town with were as loyal as what could be expected from a bunch of bandits, he still needed a few more for the next big heist.

Bull was the muscle. He was Shorty's personal bodyguard and best friend.

Cobra, Whip, and Trapper were three brothers he had met during a small-town bank robbery a few years back. They had been tied up and sitting on the ground waiting to be transported for trial, but Shorty had cut them loose and recruited them for his job. Together, they had made off with over eight thousand dollars in cash.

The other two men in his gang were Mad-Dog and Jessie. Both of them were ex-bounty hunters that ended up on the wrong side of the law after an illegal-firearms deal with a crooked sheriff went belly up.

Shorty walked over to the table where his men sat with their hats tilted low and their backs to the wall. Wanted men never left their backs exposed or their hands far from their guns. If they did, they were soon to be cannon fodder for the next man in line.

No, his men was sharp-eyed and cold-blooded.

"See anybody worth talkin' to?" Shorty asked Bull.

"Three men from the railroad crew are sittin' away from the others in that corner over there." Bull nodded his head in the direction of the men he spoke of.

The three men looked twitchy—like they were up to something. Which was exactly the sort of men Shorty was looking for. Two of the men appeared to be Chinese, which wasn't uncommon for the railway. The man with them seemed to speak their language enough to communicate openly.

Shorty tapped Cobra on the shoulder. "Go talk to the gentleman in the middle. See if they're lookin' for a way outta their contracts."

Cobra smirked and went to speak with the workers.

Shorty leaned across the table and announced, "This ain't gonna be our usual job, boys. We can't keep doin' the same thing, 'cause sooner or later they gonna catch up. The Denver & Rio Grande Western Railroad is expandin' the rails again, which is why all of these workers are here in town.

"But these boys gotta get paid, right? So they are transportin' the payroll car on a passenger train in a few days. It will make three stops before it reaches Denver to grab the passengers and then at least one more stop on its way toward Aspen. Four of y'all will be gettin' on that train in the next town after you clean yourselves up a bit."

"Where will everybody else be?" Whip asked before he threw back a shot of whiskey.

"It's gonna be Bull, Mad-Dog, Jessie, and Cobra on the train. Our dear friend William S. Jackson—the president of DRGW—will have upped the security on board after all the jobs we've done in the last couple of years. So we need men on the inside that can control the situation," Shorty explained. "Whip, you and I are gonna be ridin' along beside the train, in case somethin' goes wrong. Trapper will wait with all the horses so we can make a clean getaway. The three workers talkin' to Cobra will set up explosives on the track, rigged to go off once we're gone. Everybody meets up at Independence Pass."

"What about the passengers?"

"No hostages this time. It's too risky. If everything goes right with the explosives, there won't be any witnesses to worry about." Shorty chuckled. "I sure would hate to miss the fireworks, though."

The boys joined him in an uproar of unruly laughter, disturbing some patrons in the bar. Blowing up a train full of people wasn't the worst thing Shorty and his crew had done. At one point, his antics had even resulted in him standing face to face with the famous bounty hunter of the people himself, Cully McCullough. Cully was the only man Shorty had ever viewed as his equal.

One day he hoped to repay the bounty hunter for the scar on his back—he got it after a shot from Cully's Winchester ripped through him like a piece of wet newspaper. For a long time, the authorities had thought Shorty bled to death after a vicious shootout. His entire gang had been gunned down, but no—Shorty had survived and decided to lie low for a few years. When everyone seemed to forget about him, he rose up out of the darkness and started robbing folks blind.

He would have stayed unrecognized if it hadn't been for a traitor in his operation. Someone he thought he could trust snitched to a ranger out in New Mexico. Shorty had dealt with the traitor, but not before the bounty had been placed on his head. A wanted man, the only thing he cared about these days was making a profit at the expense of the Denver & Rio Grande Western Railroad.

Them boys were too rich for their own good. It was only fair to spread that wealth around a little.

He went over the plan in his head again.

Mad-Dog, Cobra, Jessie, and Bull would spread out through the different cars. Jessie and Cobra had to carry the tools they would need on board to break into the car holding the safe and the payroll. Keeping everyone hidden among the regular folk would be their only way of staying unnoticed until the time was right.

Going in guns blazing would only get them all in trouble.

Bull needed to take out whatever armed guards were holed up on the train. Whether it was one or an entire army, Bull had the fighting abilities to take them out with no problem whatsoever.

Jessie had to drop the tool bags and leave Cobra with the safe in the private car to join Mad-Dog and Bull. The three of them were instructed to keep an eye on the passengers until all the money was secured.

Shorty and Whip would ride beside the train as an added threat from the outside.

Trapper was instructed to wait with the horses at a halfway mark a few miles outside of Aspen. If the train stopped to let them get off, Trapper would ride out to inform the miners to blow the tracks up. Using explosives would have made it look like an accident at the mining camps rather than an intentional diversion or a way to cover their trail. If the train didn't stop, Trapper was to assume everyone on board had died or been captured and head to Independence Pass to wait for any survivors to show up.

After all of his men were given instructions, Shorty mounted his horse and pulled up beside the railway. He rode along the track under the cover of night, calculating every possible outcome, weighing the odds of their success.

This had been his ritual for the past three nights.

He mapped out his plan over and over, adding several contingency tactics if unexpected elements were introduced during the heist. Shorty was nothing if not prepared. Some may view his actions as too cautious or paranoid, but when hunting prey, it was always best to think ten steps ahead.

There weren't many structures between the last passenger stop and Aspen. It would be the perfect place for an ambush. No way to alert the authorities and no chances of being seen by anyone who wasn't on the train. Opportunities to hit a payroll car were rare, so they needed to work fast.

Independence Pass was marked on his map as well. Heavily wooded mountain terrain with thin trails, forgotten roads, and not a person in sight unless they didn't want to be found. He remembered when his father used to tell him stories of hunting wild game in the area. Before the railroads and settlements invaded the wildernesses of Colorado, all the land was as untamed as Independence Pass.

Shorty folded the map, reached into the saddlebag, and removed his hand-rolled cigarettes. He struck the sulfur tip of a match and lit the end of his cigarette before placing it in his mouth. Orange light glowed each time he inhaled and smoke puffed through his nostrils as he exhaled. He rolled his tongue around his mouth to taste the soothing bite of tobacco.

He would have preferred a cigar, but those would have to wait until the celebration. If his men did not make it out alive in time to escape toward Independence Pass, he intended to watch the embers fall from the sky as it all burned. Bull pulled his horse up beside Shorty and looked out over the landscape. He seemed a bit hesitant to blow up the train, but it was the only way to ensure they wouldn't be identified or followed by whatever security William S. Jackson had hired on.

"What's got you so quiet?" Shorty asked.

"There's a lot of room for error, even with a plan like yours. We ain't never been caught, but we've come close. It's only a matter of time before our luck runs dry."

"Don't believe in luck." Shorty took a long drag on his cigarette. "Luck don't exist, Bull. Only people too stupid to see what's happenin' around them believe in luck. And I know you ain't as stupid as you look to be."

"No, I ain't stupid. I just think we're takin' an unnecessary risk with blowin' up the train." Bull looked down at his hands. They were rough and mangled from all the fights he had been in. Like Shorty, he was a broken man.

They were all broken men.

"Not unnecessary when you consider who the armed guards might be on board. The suits that run the DRGW wouldn't risk losin' all of that money. Not to mention, y'all gonna be outnumbered by the passengers and won't stand a chance if any of them decide to play hero. We have to be prepared for whatever they throw our way. No more messes." Shorty took one last drag before stamping out the cigarette on the tip of the saddle horn. "You ain't never questioned me like this before. What's changed?"

"Just promise me you won't blow up the train if there ain't a need to," Bull pleaded. It was completely out of character for him to be so worried about something. Perhaps that little wife of his was softening the big man up. In that case, it might be best if the train robbery was the last job Bull did with Shorty.

"You ain't serious! What the heck has Mary done to you, Bull? Since when do we care about blowin' things up?"

"You just goin' back to the old ways again, and it got everybody we knew killed. Stop doin' the same things that got you caught the last time! Do you really want to add more to your bounty?" Bull looked desperate. "Cully is still out there somewhere. I read about him in the papers. And we won't know if he's on our trail until it's too late."

"Why do you think I'm doin' this? You think I'm out here to play in the dang snow?" Shorty shouted. "This is the biggest job we've ever pulled off, and you know we won't be able to stay in Colorado when it's over. We got to split up and go our separate ways. But on that train, I need you on my side."

"Please, Louis," Bull begged. "Don't get Cully on our trail because you want to be a dang fool and over think everythin'. I want to live long enough to spend the money we've saved up."

Shorty hated whenever Bull found a conscience. There was too much at stake for him to be questioned over every decision he made. But for a friend and a loyal partner, he would agree, even if he really didn't want to. "Fine. We won't blow up the train unless we have to. But if things start to turn sour, I won't hesitate to do it. Just make sure you're off the train when it happens. Don't make me bring bad news home to Mary."

"If it happens, I'll be gone."

Shorty nudged his horse into motion and continued down the track with Bull. He missed the days when they were young and willing to raise hob for no more than a few coins in their pockets. Times were changing, and Shorty wanted nothing to do with the new world ahead.

Chapter 3

Cully stoked the fire as he hummed, the sound rumbling deep in his chest. Snow fell softly outside his window and painted the landscape in the purest white he had ever seen. He was dressed casually in a simple shirt and a pair of pants. Cully preferred comfort to style most of the time.

He had bathed and shaved before sitting down with his coffee to relax against the settee in the foyer. Beside him was a pile of letters. Some of them were from people he had helped in the past, kind folk just looking to restate their respect and gratitude. But among the masses of flattering letters and telegrams were various handwritten notes from Maria Rodriguez. They were short one sentence notes, but they were filled with compassion.

Make sure you are taking care of yourself, Samuel.

One of his personal favorites was so much like Maria he could almost hear her voice as he read it quietly to himself.

If you die out there because you want to be stubborn, I will bring you back to life just to kill you myself.

Maria and the others he had met during one of his more recent jobs had become like family. He thought of them fondly as he placed the letters back into the small box where he kept them. They made the quiet of his home feel more comfortable than before when it had been filled with the emptiness that had once echoed through the halls.

The hard life on the trail made a man dream of warmth and softness. Invitations to winter socials kept arriving at the telegram office in Durango, but he had no intentions of attending that sort of thing. Grace and Wesley's wedding had been bad enough. He had walked into the small church smelling like gunpowder and the wrong end of a horse.

No, socials weren't his thing. Crowds in general were not his idea of a good time. But sitting by a fire, alone with his thoughts, in the comfort of his home was the closest thing to heaven Cully had ever experienced. When a man had been shot at and carved up with as many blades as he had, he needed the quiet no matter how much he feared it.

Other men hid from their demons—it was why outlaws felt the need to cause so much trouble—but Cully tamed his. He wouldn't let the nightmares of watching his parents die or the guilt of taking lives cloud the way he viewed his purpose. If he did, it would cripple him, and Samuel McCullough was not a man who frightened easily.

But he enjoyed these moments of peace.

Sure, it was only a matter of time before a job came knocking on his door or a contract showed up at the telegram office, but his home was his sanctuary for the time being.

Cully stood up and grabbed his jacket, pulled on his boots, and headed out to the stable to feed Samson before they would be heading into town for supplies. A storm was coming, and he didn't want to be unprepared if they got snowed in. Samson was happy to see him when he walked into the stable. His long tail flicked back and forth.

Cully lit an oil lamp that waited just beside the doors and carried it over to see his horse in the light. He smiled brightly at Samson and brushed a hand over his shiny coat. The short hairs were soft against his calloused palm. Samson was happy to be home, too, it seemed.

There wasn't a better piece of horseflesh to be found in all the four corner states.

He fed Samson his oats and a bit of sweet potatoes. Later, he could have some fruit, but they had to purchase some from a merchant in town first. Cully sang to Samson as he saddled him up, the two of them were the best of friends and the fiercest companions.

The seven miles to Durango was short but freezing cold as the temperature dropped. Most of the people in town avoided the streets when it got that cold, but if he wanted to make it back home before the storm hit, he didn't really have much of a choice in the matter.

Cully hated tying off Samson outside in that sort of weather. "Be good now and keep yourself warm," he whispered.

The bell above the door of the telegram office chimed upon his entrance. Cully rubbed his hands together and walked over to the operator expectantly. The short, portly man behind the desk looked at him over a pair of wire-framed spectacles.

"Mr. McCullough, just in time," the man said eagerly before handing over his telegrams. Several of them were the usual contract offers, most of which wouldn't be worth his effort. He would leave those for the bounty hunters struggling to find work. But among the massive stack of contracts was one that caught his attention. The telegram was from William S. Jackson, the president of the Denver & Rio Grande Western Railroad.

It was an offer for twenty dollars a day to ride their trains, plus a bonus of two thousand dollars for capturing a man named Louis "Shorty" Gerhard. They suspected Mr. Gerhard was the train raider behind their recent robberies.

The name sounded familiar, but Cully couldn't quite place it in his memory. William S. Jackson's telegram also stated that the company would pay for all travel expenses if Cully left for Denver that night. "Guess I'll be waiting out the storm on the next train out of here."

"Safe travels, Mr. McCullough."

"Thank you. Have a good evening," Cully responded. He walked out of the telegram office and went to grab Samson. It looked like his downtime had come to an early end, so it was time to get to work. The offer was sound, and the money was generous, so there was no need to turn it down. Especially when he needed the money for sprucing up the farm.

They arrived at the train station a few minutes later where Cully loaded Samson onto the livery car and boarded the passenger coach.

———

William S. Jackson's office was exactly what Cully would have expected from the president of a railroad company. An oversized oak desk sat in the center of a room that was wrapped in clean brick walls. On those walls hung photographs and certificates. The wooden floors were professionally done, crafted from rare planks of various grains. Leather wingback chairs faced the desk. It would have been subtler if he had just stood on the mount and screamed, "I am an important person."

Even so—no matter how flamboyant the man may have been—he still needed Cully's help.

A young lady came into the office a few seconds later, carrying a tray of coffee cups. The spoons on the tray rattled as her hands shook, her thin arms struggling with the weight. Cully jumped to his feet and relieved her of her burden, an act that earned him a bashful smile from the young lady.

Cully set the tray down on the table beside one of the wingback chairs. William S. Jackson came into the room not too long after the young lady. "Kara, would you excuse Mr. McCullough and I?" he asked.

"Yes, sir."

When the girl was out of the room, Cully got the sense that the situation was more serious than the telegram had implied. If the job was to ride the train and bring in Louis Gerhard why hold a meeting instead of sending a second telegram?

"Mr. McCullough, I have heard of your reputation, and I think that you are the only man capable of taking down the criminal operation that has been raiding my trains. Shorty rides with six outlaws." William S. Jackson handed Cully a stack of wanted posters of men who could be working with Louis Gerhard. "But don't worry, we'll have six hired guns on board with you. The train I am most concerned about is the one carrying the payroll for the railway workers."

Cully nodded his head and listened. The train would be ripe for the picking if it were running toward the mining camps in the mountains near Aspen. There was talk of the railroad companies blowing holes in the rock to expand the railway.

"If somebody told him about the payroll cart, he'll be hittin' that one for sure. No need to worry about the other trains," Cully stated. "He ain't like the outlaws I'm used to huntin'. Most of them weren't playin' with a full deck, if you catch my meanin'. He seems smart and calculating."

"Which is exactly why we need your help, Mr. McCullough. Shorty is a very intelligent man and as mean as a rattlesnake. You are the only one capable of bringing down his operation and stopping the crimes against my company."

"How does he usually operate?"

"They've hurt us in many ways. They usually stop the trains by laying out large trees across the tracks, blowing up the trestles before the train can arrive, boulders, a herd of cattle, you name it. His plans are unpredictable, but they always work." William S. Jackson took a moment to sip his coffee while Cully flipped through the stack of posters. "When the trains stop, the bandits board and take what they can from the passengers and the mail car. They usually hit the safe in the company's private car the hardest, leaving nothing behind but dead bodies and empty bags."

If any of the men on the posters were working with Louis Gerhard, the train ride was going to be quick and bloody. He recognized two of the men on the posters. Mad-Dog and Jessie Elliott were ex-bounty hunters who used to work in

Arizona. At the time, Mad-Dog was known as Roscoe Waller. Raiding trains was right up their alley.

The other men on the posters were Maurice "Bull" Burton and the three Holloway brothers, Theodore "the Trapper" Holloway, Christopher "the Cobra" Holloway, and Emmett "the Whip" Holloway.

"Any hostages?" Cully asked, hoping this job didn't end up like the last one. All the men had criminal records that could span the entire length of Cully's body, which was well over six feet tall, and no good for anyone who would be on that train. The faces that looked up from the posters were capable of the violence and crimes they were accused of.

"They take fewer hostages with each robbery. Shorty doesn't like witnesses, which is why we suspected him in the first place. The men in his gang are fond of taking a girl, here and there, but it hasn't happened in a while. The only one that survived being held hostage is still here in Denver. She's the reason we were able to narrow down our search. I'm sure you'll meet her soon."

"The trains are stopped in the middle of nowhere, halfway to their destination. No witnesses, no way of identifying the masked robbers, and no money left on the train. But this one girl gets away from six armed men with experience that rivals my own?" Cully asked skeptically. "It ain't strikin' you as suspicious that they know which trains are carryin' the safe and the payroll every time?"

"Indeed, which is why I need you and the other hired guns on board to make sure these things don't happen again. The next payroll train leaves Denver next Thursday morning. You and the other men I employed will have to come up with a plan that won't end with everybody getting killed."

He could have walked away and denied the contract, but he didn't. If what William S. Jackson said was true, these men needed to be stopped. Cully didn't know who the hired guns were that he would be working with, but he hoped they were ready to face off with a group of highly skilled and highly intelligent outlaws.

Chapter 4

Cully heard he could find the hired guns in a bordello on Market Street. His mother would have been rolling around in her grave if she knew he had set foot in a place like that. While there was no wrong in the way those men and women were conducting business, it just wasn't his way of life.

Sure enough, he spotted five men being served drinks by a couple of the working girls. Cully approached them and nodded his head in greeting. "You wouldn't happen to be some of the gentlemen working for Mr. William S. Jackson, would you?" he inquired.

"We are. And who might you be?" one of the men asked.

"My name is Samuel McCullough, but most folks know me best as Cully." That glimmer of recognition in their eyes was enough to let him know just how renowned his reputation had made him. It happened more and more often with each job. At one time, only criminals and lawmen knew his name.

"I'm Wolf, and the man to my left is my cousin Midnight. The other men are Jake Rider, Leo Bray, and Isaac Finley."

"I was told there would be six men," Cully said.

The men smiled at Cully's words, as though there was an inside joke that he wasn't a part of. He quirked his eyebrow at Wolf and tilted his head to the side. Cully didn't like being taken for a fool.

"Charlotte Dean isn't a man." Wolf laughed. "But she sure as heck fights like one. Be careful around her, my friend. She looks just as beautiful as she is lethal, and she bites when she's angry. Don't say I didn't warn you."

At first, Cully thought Wolf was just pulling his leg, but the man rolled up his sleeve to show a distinctive bite mark on his forearm.

"You boys whining about me again?"

He turned around and was struck by the sight of Miss Charlotte Dean. Her long, blonde hair fell like a river of golden silk past her waist. Riveting blue eyes, as clear as the summer day, held an ice in their gaze that rivaled the snow outside.

"No whining, Charlotte. Just warning our new friend here."

"You had that bite coming, and you know it." Miss Dean removed her hat and sat beside Jake Rider. "That's what awaits any man who cheats at poker and tries to steal my winnings."

While Cully had been shocked by how little it took to provoke her, the other men laughed in memory of the disagreement over said poker winnings. "My name is Samuel McCullough, Miss Dean."

"I know who you are, Cully. Could tell by the way you walked in like you owned the place. Please, call me Charlotte," she said before leaning back in her seat, her mouth curling into a smile. "Although, if you keep staring at me with those pretty eyes, I might just let you call me whatever you like."

Cully felt his face heat up as he glanced away, turning six shades of red.

Charlotte snickered mischievously. She gave him a sassy wink when he looked back at the group. "So what's the plan?"

He cleared his throat before answering. "You all know who we're goin' after, so I won't pour honey on the situation just so it's easier to swallow. We each bring guns and board the train before the passengers. Check for explosives and spread out into the different cars. Watch everyone that comes on board but be subtle. On the ride, we'll be searchin' for signs of activity. If Louis Gerhard is as unpredictable as our employer believes, he'll be indirect and hit us when we least expect it."

"Some of us will need to stay close to the safe in the company car," Midnight inserted. Wolf and Midnight began to argue over who would stay with the safe.

Charlotte ignored their bantering and spoke directly to Cully. "I know Shorty. I've been following him for three years. Every train he's hit, I was only one step behind. It's why I'm here. He killed a friend of mine for turning him over to the authorities in New Mexico. So far, it sounds like your plan will work, but we need to think of every possible outcome. He's worse than the company thinks."

"You're the girl they held hostage, ain't you?" Cully asked.

"Yes. I was on the right train, and for once, I thought I had him. We were finally in the same place at the same time. They were outnumbered, and Shorty knew that. He and his gang wore masks and ordered everybody to get on the floor.

A few of the passengers got a little brave and pulled out guns. Shorty went mad, started threatening to hurt people, so I threw myself at his feet, and he took the bait."

"What happened?"

"A lot could happen to a girl in the time I was with them." Charlotte glanced away. "He took me to make sure they had something to bargain with in case the lawmen came knocking at their hideout. They weren't like the other outlaws I came across. The hideout was clean and nice."

"How'd you get away, Charlotte?"

"After Cobra verbally abused me with threats—not for information, just for a bit of fun—they rode out to attack a stagecoach. Shorty said they needed the money for their next job." Charlotte looked away from Cully again and folded her hands in her lap. "They left Cobra behind to have his fun, but the cowards never expected me to fight back. I knew it was my only chance to get away."

Cully had heard stories like Charlotte's countless times, but there was something about the situation that didn't add up. Someone had been feeding information to Louis Gerhard, and that person just might be Charlotte. He would have to keep an eye on her. "What can you tell me about Shorty that the company doesn't know?"

She appeared to think about her answer, looking to her comrades for support. "The stagecoaches and other jobs are just to fund the train robberies. I'm sure you noticed how little the company actually knows about Shorty. He usually uses the same methods if it's just a regular passenger train. But he never hits the payroll trains the same way twice."

"Which is why they don't have a straight answer on what we should expect when we get on that train," Cully reasoned.

"Exactly."

Wolf turned toward Cully and offered him a seat, but Cully decided it would be best to discuss the intricacies of their plan in a more private location. He planned for them to meet at a local inn after he sent a telegram.

The telegram was to a friend in New Mexico who worked for the state authorities. It was a request to launch an investigation into Charlotte Dean and her involvement with Louis "Shorty" Gerhard. Not many criminals with Gerhard's intelligence would have let a witness just disappear.

Any witness would have been hunted down, or the criminal would have gone underground, but Louis Gerhard had continued to attack the trains owned by the Denver & Rio Grande Western Railroad. Charlotte was a loose end, but it seemed like the gang wasn't too worried about her.

Cully had seen operations fall apart over less.

Charlotte and the others met in Cully's rented room at the local inn, but he arrived several minutes after they did. He shook the snow out of his jacket and hung it on a hook beside the door along with his old hat.

"Who's Maria?" Charlotte asked suddenly. She stood beside the dresser with a few letters in her hands.

"She's a friend of mine."

"You travel with her letters. You sure she's just a friend?"

The questions sort of irked Cully and chafed against his nerves, but he answered honestly. "Maria saved my life. Her letters keep me humble. They remind me that even though I put myself in danger, I'm not expendable."

No one asked any more questions, and Cully didn't offer any more answers. He flopped into a chair in the corner and looked at the group of hired guns he would be working with over the next week.

The Indians, Wolf and Midnight, were watchful. They stared out the window like something out there was staring back. Jake Rider would have been no help in the discussion; he was passed out on the bed. Isaac Finley was a man of few words. He sat on the floor, leaning against the wall.

Leo Bray walked through the door a few moments later, shivering from the ongoing storm outside. "Dang it all! Ain't been a winter this cold in years. Snow nearly put me in an early grave."

"Glad you could finally join us," Midnight said sarcastically. "We aren't in the middle of anything important."

"I don't wanna hear anything you got to say!"

"All right, enough," Cully interrupted. "I'll be in the passenger areas makin' sure everyone is safe. We'll all have a path to walk on the train, but we have exits and entrances to cover. It'll be a lot of work keepin' sharp but not alertin' the passengers of any real threat. Keepin' people safe is the only thing that matters, even if they get the money."

Leo sat on the floor beside Isaac. The group listened closely as Cully stood up from the chair.

"You all seem like a tight group, and here I am gettin' a cut of the action. I don't react well to betrayal, so if I even see thoughts of mutiny cross your minds, you'll be eatin' lead," he stated. "I'll fight beside you if you fight beside me. If you do something suspicious, I'll take you down along with the gang."

"Like you said, we're a tight group," Wolf started. "We have every reason to be suspicious, as you do. Your reputation might be one we've all heard, but in our line of work... we've been burned more times than we've been saved, my friend."

"You've read my letters, so you know the lengths I'm willin' to go to in order to protect those loyal to me. I'm not askin' for your loyalty. I'm only askin' that you do the job you were hired to do and nothin' more." Cully left the inn and went to check on Samson. He didn't bother grabbing his things; they had already done whatever digging they thought was necessary. The only thing left to do was wait.

———

Thursday morning had come, and the train carrying the large payroll was preparing to leave Denver. Cully and the other hired guns searched through each of the compartments for any sort of explosives or stowaways.

They found nothing.

Cully's anxiety eased slightly, and he motioned for the travelers to begin boarding the train. When everyone was in their seats and their tickets verified, he took a seat near the exit of a passenger car.

It was surprising how well he blended in with the crowd. The other hired guns stood out among the well-dressed commuters. He assumed that subtly was not in their nature.

Some passengers seemed to sigh in relief upon seeing them. The rumors of the train attacks had a lot of people nervous. Soft voices whispering to his right drew his attention to a cluster of giggling ladies.

One of them blushed and waved coyly. The other three were whispering among each other and pointing in Cully's direction.

"Ugh... Mornin', ladies."

They didn't reply to him directly, but he could overhear their conversation. "It ain't every day that us girls get to look upon such a fine specimen of masculinity," one of them said. The lady who had waved to him nearly caused Cully to fall over from shock.

"True, I was ready to make a fool out of myself just get him to smile a bit."

"And did you see the way he walked over here?"

Unable to handle their conversation and the flirtatious winks, he attempted to make a clean exit. But he ended up blushing like a randy schoolboy and stumbling over his tongue. "I need to... ugh, to do my... my rounds. If you ladies will excuse me."

Chapter 5

Embarrassed, Cully moved into the next car and away from the suggestive stares of the women. There were several families crowded into the seats. Couples, elderly people, mothers traveling with their children, and an occasional businessman here and there—several dozen people were crammed into the passenger cars.

A wobbly toddler stood up on a seat not far from where Cully was standing. The boy was trying to get a look at the wild horses running outside. A crooked cowboy hat was barely balanced on his head. When the child nearly toppled to the floor, Cully flipped him in the air before settling him back in the seat beside his older sister. The gleeful squeal and slobbery smile warmed his heart.

"Keep an eye on him. Can't trust the ones who wear a cowboy hat," he told the little girl, giving her a wink and tipping his own hat in her direction.

She chuckled and leaned against her mother's side.

The woman beamed up at him as chubby little fingers reached for him. "He wants you to pick him up," she clarified.

Cully reddened and reached down to lift the boy onto his shoulder. The child played with the brim of his hat for several seconds as Cully bounced him up and down a few times.

The child's mother said, "His name is Billy."

Cully smiled, nodded, and handed the toddler back to his mother. When he was confident the boy would stay put, he continued down the aisle. An elderly man was having trouble getting to the area where his granddaughter waited, so Cully supported the gentleman's weight and helped him sit down.

"Thank you, young man."

"It was no trouble, sir," he responded. Once again, he caught the way the young women on the train looked at him and quickly turned to leave. The man's granddaughter had looked at Cully as though he hung the moon.

It was then that an older couple near the back of the passenger car recognized him—not by his reputation, but from his childhood. "You wouldn't be Benjamin McCullough's boy, would you?" the man asked.

"I am. My name is Samuel McCullough, sir."

Tears glistened in the man's eyes as he squeezed his wife's hand tightly. Her eyes were just as damp as her husband's. Cully removed his hat and shook the man's hand.

"You probably don't remember us, but we used to attend the sermons at your father's church. My name is Arthur Hamish, and this is my wife, Betty."

"Pleasure, ma'am." Cully nodded his head politely.

"It's a tragedy what happened to your parents. We've kept you in our prayers over the years. Betty even collects the sections in the paper with your name in them."

"Stop that right now, Arthur." Betty swatted at Arthur, her cheeks bright. Cully was humbled by their kindness. "What are you doing on the train, Sammy?"

He slightly cringed at one of the childhood nicknames the ladies at his father's church used to call him. "I was hired to make sure that the train arrives safely. The railway has had some trouble with bandits, so they're takin' some precautions."

"Well, we feel a lot safer knowing you're here."

"Enjoy your ride," he said. As much as he was thankful for their compassion, Cully didn't want to listen to musings of his parents or pity from people who were aware of his past.

Charlotte entered the passenger cart to update him. "You here to work or break hearts, cowboy? There were a few ladies back there giving me the death look for just saying your name."

"Has anybody seen anythin' suspicious since we came aboard? There's only a few hours before we get to the most likely ambush spot."

"Midnight and Isaac are with the safe. The rest of us are spread out through the train, like you said. No one has seen anything out of the ordinary," Charlotte whispered. "I'm getting nervous, Cully. There are a lot of children onboard. Shorty isn't the sort to care if they get caught in the crossfire."

"We need to make sure that we keep the situation under control so that doesn't happen. I'm about to make the announcements. Stay safe, Charlotte."

Cully made rounds through the cars letting everyone know that the railway had hired more security to ensure their safe arrival in Aspen. He even swallowed his pride and approached the women who had been whispering about him earlier. "We're coming up on an area known for ambushes, but there's no need to be alarmed. The Denver & Rio Grande Western Railroad has hired me and a few others onboard for your added protection."

They seemed grateful for his honesty and even comforted by his presence. The truth was, until he knew what he was up against, he wouldn't allow himself to relax. He was out of his element on this contract, and he was man enough to admit it. Cully made his way toward the back of the passenger car and sat near the exit.

Behind him was the door leading to the dining car where Wolf was keeping an eye on things. Leo was in the mail car, Charlotte was covering the sleeping car, and Jake was in the baggage car. Every major area of the train was covered.

The engineer had been informed of the situation upon departure, so he knew not to stop the train unless it was necessary. He was determined to make sure that the people on the train survived.

Bull heard the passengers whispering about Cully McCullough. He had even seen him with his own eyes as the bounty hunter spoke to everyone about the security on the train. Cully was every outlaw's worst nightmare, and now Bull knew why. He thoroughly checked every passenger car with the sharpest gaze Bull had ever seen.

Cully needed to be taken care of first.

The large man stood up from his seat. His usual garb had been replaced by a nice waistcoat and jacket. All of Shorty's men on the train were disguised as travelers, their guns hidden from view in satchels. Bull's hand hovered just above his Colt as he waited for Mad-Dog's signal. When it came, he jumped to his feet with his gun drawn. He pressed it against Cully's head and barked, "You move, and they all die. Drop the gun and slide it to my friend over there. And no sudden moves."

Chaos erupted, and the passengers began to scream. Gunshots came from another area of the train. Cobra and Jesse Elliott must have taken out the two hired guns near the safe.

Shorty had been correct to assume that security had been increased since the last robbery, but he would be spitting fire when he found out Cully was among them.

Jessie entered the car, wiping blood off of his hands. He kicked Cully as he passed by before picking up the famous Winchester the outlaw always carried. "Looky here, boys. We got ourselves a bounty hunter. Don't look so tough kneelin' on the ground, do ya?"

A child near the front of the car began to cry, so Jessie fired three shots into the roof to shut everyone up. The mother of the small boy placed her hand over her screaming child's mouth, shaking with fear.

"No one move, or we start shootin—"

The second those words came out of Jessie's mouth, a strikingly familiar blonde woman came barreling through the door firing two pistols. Bull grabbed Cully and shoved him to the floor with the gun still pressed against his head. The bounty hunter trembled with rage.

Jessie fired Cully's rifle, spraying the entire passenger car with bullets. People ducked for cover, but a few weren't lucky enough to hide in time. Blood spilled over the floor and soaked Bull's boots.

The woman hadn't been aware of Mad-Dog standing behind her until the outlaw knocked her out using the end of his gun. "How many of you are there?" Bull asked Cully.

"Why don't you dive headfirst off the side of a mountain?"

"We'll see how funny you are when you're tied up and they kill everybody on this train." Bull pulled a long section of rope from beneath his jacket and secured Cully's hands behind his back, rendering the bounty hunter useless. Two more hired guns came rushing through the door. There had to be at least five outlaws so far.

Jessie shot the first one between the eyes once he passed the opening. The second one was gunned down by Mad-Dog. Bull went to instruct the locomotive engineer to stop the train. When the man refused, Bull revealed that there were explosives at the end of the track, and if the train didn't stop, everyone on board would die.

As much as he hated making Shorty angry, Bull had no intentions of blowing up a train full of children. He had seen enough death at the hands of his gang to know when things had gotten out of control. The situation was ideal—except for Cully being aboard the train. Everything had been going according to plan.

Bull returned to the passenger car as Shorty pulled his horse up beside the train and came aboard with Whip. Bull decided not to tell Shorty that Cully was on board but to wait until Shorty saw him on his own.

———————

Shame filled Cully's heart as he watched Louis "Shorty" Gerhard's gang threaten and abuse the passengers. Tied up and lying facedown on the floor, Cully had never been so embarrassed in his life. He had promised them all that they would be safe under his protection. Already the D&RG's extra protection had dwindled down to two hired guns.

Charlotte lay unconscious on the ground, and Wolf sat tied up beside her, distraught over the death of his cousin. It had been a massacre. Several passengers had been caught in the crossfire. So many people panicked when Charlotte and the outlaws opened fire on one another. The only comfort was the sound of Billy's cries, an indication that the toddler had not been injured during the gunfight.

Cully looked up at the weeping little girl who held her baby brother. Their mother still tried to shield them from the cruelty of the men on board. In moments of crisis, people tended to protect what mattered most.

They should never have stopped. Nothing could keep the gang from killing everyone.

One of the raiders that had been riding beside the train came aboard. Charlotte blinked open her eyes and looked up into the newcomer's face.

"Tell your brother Charlotte Dean is on the train," she said between shuddering breaths. "Cobra will want to see me. Let everyone else go, and I'll come with you without a fight."

At the mention of his brother's name, Emmett "the Whip" Holloway left to check on the safe.

That meant that the other men onboard were indeed Maurice "Bull" Burton, Roscoe "Mad-Dog" Waller, Jesse Elliott, and Christopher "the Cobra" Holloway.

Another man came into the passenger car. He wore a mask, but Cully could tell by the way he sauntered through the aisle that Louis "Shorty" Gerhard himself had joined the robbery.

The only member of the gang that was missing was the third Holloway brother, Theodore "the Trapper."

Cobra entered the passenger car and rushed over to Charlotte. He struck her hard across the face before he lifted her off the floor by her throat. "That was for shootin' me!" he screamed.

Charlotte was tough. She tossed her hair out of her face and stared Cobra down. "And here I thought you might have missed me while I was gone."

"What do you want?"

"Leave everybody else alone and take me with you. I know you've been looking for revenge, so now is your chance. Grab the money and take me hostage again. If you promise to leave here without hurting anybody, I promise I won't fight you." Charlotte's offer was dangerous. He hadn't known her for long, but putting herself back in the care of the man who had tortured her was both foolish and brave.

Cobra turned back to the man Cully had identified as Shorty. When the man nodded his head, Cobra hauled Charlotte off the train and threw her over the back of a horse. Wolf began to cause a ruckus, but the look in Cully's eyes forced him to be quiet. There was no use in him dying today too.

It all happened so quickly.

The gang cleaned out the safe, ransacked the baggage car, and robbed every nook and cranny they could find. There was no way of guessing just how much they got away with.

When they turned their backs, Cully tried to struggle free of his constraints. His belt buckle scraped against the floor, causing Shorty to turn around and stare directly at him. Cully began to worry when recognition flared in the outlaw's gaze.

Chapter 6

Shorty could not believe his eyes. Tied up on the floor of the passenger car was the one and only Cully McCullough. While the others took off in the direction of the rendezvous location with Charlotte Dean and the loot, Shorty knelt beside Cully's wriggling body.

"Well, well, well… Been years since I saw you," he taunted.

"Do I know you?"

"Nearly killed me a few years back, but at the time I was just a lackey for another gang. After I recovered from the hole you put in my back, I started my own operation." Shorty spread his arms wide, gesturing to the damage that had been wrought. "Pretty successful, if you ask me. Took care of them friends of yours and got away without a hitch."

"You sort never seem to know when to shut up."

Shorty landed a hefty blow across Cully's jaw. A child screamed a few seats toward the front of the passenger car.

"Be smart and keep your mouth shut. Wouldn't want to kill you in front of your biggest fan. No, I want you to live with the shame of knowin' that you failed." Shorty smiled coyly and said, "Best get moving. Wouldn't want them boys to get any funny ideas about who's in charge. You folks enjoy the rest of your trip into town."

He exited the train and climbed into the saddle. The boys weren't too far ahead, so he caught up rather quickly. Bull looked on edge.

"Don't worry. I didn't kill anybody. Just took a moment to chat with an old pal."

"What about the explosives?"

"Give me what you're carryin' and head on to the camp. Tell them workers their services are no longer required—and they ain't gettin' paid neither." Shorty waved him off after receiving the bags of money. There had been more cash on the train than his informant had mentioned.

The gang rode to the checkpoint and joined up with Trapper. Everybody got on his own horse and beat a fast retreat toward Independence Pass. Charlotte had yet to speak since Cobra took her hostage.

Despite what the group thought, Shorty wasn't too fond of hostages. They were a liability, but Charlotte—Charlotte was special for some reason. Perhaps it was the rebellious streak in her. He wanted to try to convince her she belonged in his gang.

The gang was in need of a strong woman. All of them were drawn to the fire in her veins and the conviction in her heart. A crooked man often yearned for nothing more than an honest woman and a healthy bank account.

"Glad to have you back with us, Miss Dean."

"Yeah, yeah. Home sweet home, Shorty."

He smiled at her dry humor. Maybe he wouldn't let Cobra torture her this time. She could provide some decent entertainment until they hit the road for the next job. "You always had a sharp tongue. I'd hate to let Cobra cut it out of that pretty little mouth of yours."

"See what happens if he tries. I said I wouldn't fight coming with you, but I said nothing about just lying down and taking a beating again," Charlotte barked.

"Fair enough. How 'bout you sweeten that tone a bit so I ain't inclined to shoot ya?"

"Any one of you that touches me will be walking with a permanent limp. Getting shot doesn't scare me and neither does dying. Do your worst, I ain't impressed."

The way she had been tossed over the back of Cobra's horse was not secure at all. She could have rolled off the side and tried to make a run for it when the opportunity came, but she made an effort to stay put and keep her word. He respected that. And he didn't respect most people.

"Nobody's gonna hurt you, Charlotte," Shorty began. "I got an offer for you, one I hope you'll be tempted to accept."

One look shut down Cobra's protests. Shorty could smell the stench of revenge wafting through the air, mingling with a distinctive scent of horse sweat. Again, revenge was not something Shorty allowed to cloud his judgment. If it had, he would have killed Cully when he had the chance.

They rode for several hours, only stopping to water the horses or munch down some jerky. It wasn't tasty, but it filled the hole in their guts until they arrived at the safe house. Their hideaway was a small cabin tucked away in the mountains.

"This ain't the same place as last time. Y'all didn't seem like the sort to move around a lot," Charlotte observed.

"We ain't. But you runnin' off made sure we couldn't stick around like we normally would have. You're the only hostage we let slip through our hands."

"You mean, I'm the only hostage you let live after seein' your faces," she countered. "I ain't stupid, Shorty. And neither are you. I know you're aware that I went back and tried to find the lot of you, hoping to get some payback."

In truth, he had known that she would hunt them down again. Heck, she'd been on their trail for years. But for some reason he could not fathom, he had let Charlotte Dean go free. The other hostages from past jobs either worked as informants or were dealt with in other ways in order to cover their tracks.

Shorty headed into the cabin and removed his boots. He placed them beside the door and hung his hat and coat up to dry. The fireplace was crackling, filling the space with warmth and comfort, which meant Valerie had decided to visit.

Valerie had taken on the name of Kara and started working as William S. Jackson's assistant at the Denver & Rio Grande Western Railroad. She had been one of the first hostages his gang had ever taken. Valerie was young and naïve, easily manipulated into doing whatever Shorty asked of her. In some ways he thought she fancied him.

"Valerie," he called.

She appeared in the doorway to the kitchen moments later. In her hands sat a hot apple pie that made his mouth water. Valerie's continued efforts to try to impress him had always been obvious.

He accepted her gift but met her gaze sternly. "I told you not to come back until after things cooled down a bit. They can't find out who you really are, *Kara*. They'll hang you out to dry in the sun."

"I know. I just wanted to make sure everyone was all right," she murmured. "And I brought you some information."

"What is it?"

"The railway company has set up an even bigger shipment on the payroll train that's supposed to be heading out of Denver in the next couple of weeks. The new year is almost here, Shorty. So this is your chance to get the money you need to leave," Valerie whispered. The longing in her eyes made his stomach turn.

Shorty hated desperate people, especially those who could not fend for themselves and relied on the strength of others to get them through life. "Take this," Shorty said, tossing one of the bags of money at her. "Go up north and change your name again. Your services are no longer required."

Valerie began to weep at his feet, but he brushed off her touch. He knew she expected to mean something to him, that he would take her with him when he left town, but no. The only personal ties Shorty had were to Bull and his wife, Mary.

And he was about to cut them out of his life as well.

———

Cully and Wolf got off the train in Aspen. Neither of the men said a word, for there was nothing to be said. They had failed miserably. The anger swirling around in Cully's mind hungered for retribution. Shorty and his gang needed to be stopped. And now that he had an idea of who the man behind the mask really was, Cully knew he could take him down.

Samson was scheduled to arrive soon, so he had a short amount of time to come up with a plan. Instead of allowing Wolf to wander off in a state of depression, Cully pulled the man along with him. They rented a room near the train station and attempted to pull themselves together.

"I promised Midnight that we would come home if he helped me with this one contract," Wolf said before taking a big swig of beer. "I never considered that one of us wouldn't make it out alive. Not after everything we had lived through."

"No one leaves home expectin' to die unless they're criminals or soldiers, so don't blame yourself for this."

"I guess hired guns are bit of a gray area, my friend— bounty hunters as well. None of us are expected to live long enough to hit thirty. It's a sad world we live in."

Wolf was right. There were some men who were forced to walk a thin line each day. Men like Jesse Elliott and Roscoe Waller where perfect examples of those who crossed that line. "We have to stop them from hittin' the next train. And we have to get Charlotte back."

"They knew we would be on that train. Shorty took our men out faster than any of us could react. He even got the jump on you, Cully. And to my knowledge that's never happened before." Wolf met Cully's gaze with unwavering determination.

"You're right. I messed up. Shouldn't have underestimated him. But this time, I ain't goin' in like a hired gun."

"Shorty must have informants within the company. What do you suggest?"

"That we forget the reward money and what the company wants. This is about retribution now and Louis Gerhard will be brought to justice by my hands only. I let him get away once, I won't make that mistake again," Cully vowed. "We take a page from his book and stage men on the train. Dressed as either passengers or members of the staff."

"You think he'll fall for that?" Wolf's words came out in a jumbled slur, but Cully could still make out most of it.

"He probably won't expect us to even try stoppin' him again so soon after what happened this mornin'. Which is why it's important that we keep this up," he explained. "Stay here and take a few days for yourself. I'm taking the next train back to Denver, then ride up to Boulder to round up a few men and find out when the next payroll train is leavin'. Meet me back in Denver in five days."

"I will gather guns and other supplies we may need."

Two days later Cully rode into Boulder, Colorado and found himself a room. He knew most of the hired guns in the area liked to stay holed up in town so they could take jobs in Denver and Fort Collins without traveling too far.

Boulder wasn't as big as some other settlements in Colorado, but there was a bit of traffic here and there when travelers came passing through. Cully took time to wash up and change clothes before heading out. He spent a long time just trying to avoid his own gaze in the mirror. Disgusted with himself, he left as fast as he could.

The utter disappointment in the eyes of Billy and the other passengers had ripped through his heart. What good was he if he couldn't bring the bad guys to justice? While Cully wasn't immune to the cunning ways of criminals, he rarely stepped into a trap—especially one he wasn't able to get out of. He failed. It was as simple as that, but that didn't mean he was just going to lie down and not set things right.

Despite the early afternoon hour, Cully found himself wandering into a bar. He saddled up and ordered a beer to calm the nagging guilt in his gut. The bartender looked at him suspiciously, but he didn't feel like explaining why he was drinking alcohol in the middle of the day. No need to rehash his most recent letdown. "Got anybody in town lookin' for work?"

The bartender said nothing, so Cully reached into his pocket and slid a bill across the bar.

"Yeah, couple of fellas came into town two nights ago. Lookin' to get hired onto some contract work. They're in the third room just up the stairs," the man admitted.

Cully slammed his beer and shuffled up the stairs. He didn't bother knocking on the door. He just swung it open and ignored the guns aiming for his head. He raised his hands.

"Heard you boys were lookin' for a job," he muttered.

All the guns were lowered but not holstered. Cully walked over and took a seat in a chair near the door, keeping his hands raised just above shoulder level. He stretched his long legs and peered at the men beneath the brim of his hat.

There were three of them, which would be plenty including Wolf and himself. One of the men walked over to him and smacked his hat off his head.

Cully jumped to his feet and stood toe to toe with Mateo Rodriguez. "What are you doin' here, Mateo?" he asked accusingly.

"I could ask you the same thing. You are lucky I did not shoot you when you walked through the door, señor."

"What does Maria think of you workin' as a hired gun?"

"I told you when I left that I had some business to take care of. Well, this is where my business has led me. Maria does not know, and I do not intend for her to find out."

Mateo looked rougher than he had at the wedding. His hair was long and matted beneath his hat. And the pathetic state of the beard covering his jaw probably meant that these men hadn't bathed in weeks. From the looks of the room, he was probably correct in his assumptions.

"Why have you come to speak with us?"

"I got a job for you, if you're interested," Cully said simply.

"What job?"

"I'm takin' down Louis "Shorty" Gerhard and his gang." Cully got straight to the point.

The men in the room let out a string of foul curses and looked at him as though he were mad.

But no, Cully wasn't crazy. He was furious. And he needed to channel that fury into his work or else he would never be able to move on from the shame.

Chapter 7

Boulder, Colorado

Cully met up with Wolf, Mateo, and his two men, Dani and James, in the room he had rented instead of meeting in Denver right away. Things were back to square one, and they needed a plan. Wolf brought guns and supplies, but it wasn't everything Cully had in mind. He threw down several bundles of clothing, razors and hair brushes. "Within these bundles are everythin' you'll need to transform yourselves into respectable citizens."

They squinted at him in confusion while he continued.

"Y'all are gonna bathe, shave, and change into these suits. Wolf will ride with the locomotive engineer, and Mateo will join me in the passenger car. The rest of you will spread out."

"What will we do when they get on board?" Wolf asked.

"We disarm them before they can hurt civilians. No one is permitted to kill any member of the gang unless disarmin' them is completely impossible without riskin' your own life or that of the passengers. Anybody who breaks this rule will be arrested under the same charges as the man he kills, are we clear?" It was harsh, maybe, but there was a difference between the unbiased retribution of justice and all out revenge.

"Do not shoot an unarmed man. If they come in guns blazin', then do what you must. We'll hide the guns throughout the train so we do not bring them on board and alert the passengers. Extra pistols and rifles will be strapped under seats in the passenger car as an added precaution. Wolf will keep his rifle with him in the locomotive. You two," he said, gesturing between Dani and James, "you will conceal your weapons and wait until Wolf gives the signal. We'll be tryin' to catch them off guard and take them down quietly."

And Cully intended to do it the right way.

"Wolf will signal the rest of us when they stop the train. You will hold your fire until they are on board and in position. They'll most likely try to run if we act too soon. Let's not scare them off but let them feel secure."

Cully paused to allow them to digest the information. When none of them raised any questions, he cleared his throat before continuing.

"Hold them at gunpoint until all the passengers are off the train and out of harm's way. Evacuating the train is vital. Do not—I repeat—do not shoot them unless they give you a reason to do so."

Wolf spoke then. "Do not underestimate anyone in this gang my friends... especially Shorty himself. He's more slippery than a tadpole in a spring river but far more lethal. Get the passengers to safety, arrest whatever outlaws are still breathing, and get paid for a successful job. It's that simple."

When everyone was briefed on the plan and no one had any more questions, Mateo and Cully went out on the porch for a cigarette. Cully didn't smoke often, he really went out mainly to catch up with a man who he had fought beside a few months back.

Mateo was much quieter than he remembered. Before, you couldn't pay to shut the man up for a few seconds. He was always joking or trying to lighten the mood in some other way; Mateo was the exact opposite of his younger sister Maria. They were strong and chaotic at the same time. Where she was all fire and seriousness, Mateo was calm as a river and amusing, even when things turned sour.

Both of the siblings had strong convictions and were compassionate with every bone in their body. Cully admired that in both of them, but he was concerned about the dangerous road Mateo was headed down.

"I don't mean to pry—"

"Then don't," Mateo interrupted. "I know what you are going to ask, but I do not have an answer for you—or anyone. At least not yet... I ask that you respect my privacy, and I shall do the same. Just know that I am not harming anyone or doing anything illegal. Everything is just..."

"Yeah. I know what you mean. But I also know what a man on the run looks like. I won't ask what you're runnin' from. I just hope you're takin' care of yourself and keepin' in touch with Maria and your mother."

Mateo looked to his boots as Cully's gut hit the floor.

"What is it?" he urged. "What aren't you tellin' me?"

"Did you not wonder why Maria hasn't been answering your letters? I went back to La Rosa, but it was burned to the ground, and Maria was gone. That was two weeks ago. Madre is safe, but where my sister is, I do not know."

"Why didn't you try to contact me?"

"You aren't the easiest person to find, señor. And for all I knew, you had forgotten about everyone after we all left the wedding. Maria hadn't mentioned you in her letters and Wesley said he hadn't seen you the day I rode through Fort Collins."

Cully wanted to pound his fists into something. He owed Maria Rodriguez his life, but he needed to finish what he had started.

Mateo read his expression and said, "A mystery for another day, perhaps. Do not worry, señor. I will find Maria."

————————

Charlotte Dean stretched like a lazy cat waking up from a long nap in the sun. She couldn't remember the last time she had slept so peacefully. Her hand brushed against soft cotton sheets as the smell of bacon wafted through the air. Her stomach grumbled, and her eyes fluttered open.

The sun was bright, glistening off the snow outside and casting a stunning light around the bedroom. She half-expected to feel pain or the bite of rope cutting into her wrists, but all she felt was peace. Had she escaped and completely forgotten? No, Charlotte recognized the room, although she wasn't being tortured like before.

Her joints creaked—a side effect from being in the saddle for days on end—as she unfolded herself from the mattress. Part of her wanted to crawl beneath the covers and pretend it was all a dream, but she knew when a man was trying to woo her. And that was exactly what Shorty had been trying to do. But she had no interest in joining up with his gang.

Charlotte tied her long hair back and walked out of the room to find Bull and Shorty playing a round of Black Jack with Mad-Dog as the dealer. It was Bull's turn. "Stand. Hit and you'll bust. Trust me," she advised. "Mad-Dog's got the cards stacked against you, looking to brown-nose Shorty a bit."

Shorty cursed and looked at Mad-Dog. "You been cheatin' to make me win? I don't know if I'm insulted or flattered."

She nudged Mad-Dog out of the way and took the dealer's seat. Charlotte shuffled the cards with expert accuracy and dealt the first hand. "We play for information, boys. I win, you fork up the details of your next plan. I lose, you can ask me whatever you like." Bold as always, Charlotte looked to Shorty. He smiled in approval and nodded his head.

"Hit."

Charlotte dealt Shorty a card.

"Stand," said Bull when his turn came.

She won when Mad-Dog and Bull fell short and Shorty bust at twenty-five. "What's the next job?"

The card game continued as Shorty thought of his answer. Charlotte waited patiently even though she wanted to scream.

"We'll be hittin' a few smaller ones for a few weeks. There's a few big payroll trains comin' up, but we'll wait until the most profitable one hits the track," Shorty responded.

"Going into the new year with a bang? Sounds a bit flashy even for you, Shorty." Charlotte dealt the next hand but lost to Mad-Dog. Shorty looked smug and leaned over the table.

"Did you sleep well?"

"You can ask me anything, and you choose to ask how I slept last night? Bit of a waste, don't you think?" she asked.

"Depends on how you look at things. Answer the question, please. Those are the terms you set."

Charlotte didn't know what to think, but she told him honestly. There was no use in lying after everything she had been through with the men in the room. There was no bond between her and Shorty or his gang, but there was a shared appreciation for skill and fortitude.

She won the next round. "Why'd you let Cully live? You told me the story of how you two met, and you had the chance to get revenge, so why didn't you take it?" For a moment Charlotte thought she had gone too far, but Shorty squared his shoulders and answered the question.

"Cully is the type of man who would welcome death. Denyin' him that privilege and forcin' him to live in shame is the best revenge I could have taken in that moment. He's cached up somewhere hatin' himself, while I live my life."

Charlotte won the next two rounds, and the game ended. She and Shorty grabbed a bottle of whiskey and some glasses. They sat down and continued their candid conversation while the others headed into town to pick up food before the next storm hit. Charlotte was eager to learn about their plans.

"So, what? You just hoping he offs himself and takes care of the dirty work for you?"

"Absolutely. Ain't no better revenge against the son of a preacher. The most legendary bounty hunter in these parts eats the end of his own rifle after an embarrassing failure that ended his career. I can just imagine the look on his face when he's forced to meet his God in the glorious halls of Heaven to confess his sins. Dang near poetic." Shorty sipped at his whiskey.

Charlotte took a swig from her own glass. "You know, I always meant to thank you," she admitted. "Heck, before you took me hostage, I was a nobody. I was a frightened, inexperienced little girl chasing the dream of avenging her friend. But you and your gang woke up something else inside of me. Without it, I would have never learned my true potential."

"Folks like to ignore the fact that crime and tragedy plays a role in shapin' who we are as people. Ain't a lawman alive who came into his job without gettin' burned first."

Charlotte raised her glass and offered a toast, "To crime and the monsters it turned us into. May we never sleep another peaceful night while our demons stalk our dreams."

Their glasses chimed.

"To crime," Shorty agreed.

Just as they emptied their glasses, the other gang members came rushing in from the cold. Cobra locked eye with Charlotte, his handsome face contorting into a wide grin.

Suddenly, she didn't feel as comfortable as she had before. Shorty placed his hand on her shoulder to stop her from trembling. Charlotte hadn't even realized she had begun to shake. Cobra removed his hat and boots before stripping off his jacket. She watched every motion, familiar with the way he moved and the way his mind worked.

After weeks of torture beneath his evil hand, she knew him more than anyone else. Charlotte Dean had been broken while witnessing the epitome of darkness within a man's soul.

"Lookin' mighty beautiful there, Charlotte Dean."

"Don't touch her, Cobra," Shorty warned.

Cobra didn't look happy about Shorty giving him orders when it came to Charlotte. "I owe her for what she did to me, Shorty. Stay out of it. This is between me and her."

The distinctive sound of a bullet sliding into the chamber of a gun caused Charlotte's heart to skip a beat. She stood up from her chair and backed against the far wall, putting some space between the hostile men in the room. They could take each other out for all she cared, but she didn't want to get caught in the crossfire when the bullets started flying.

"She shot me!" Cobra protested.

"Unlike her, I'll shoot you dead. I ain't in the mood to be dealin' with your foolishness. Charlotte is a guest. I didn't agree to bring her along so you could play your sick games." Shorty's calm façade never wavered under pressure.

"You goin' soft, Shorty?" the other man accused. "Ain't like you to stand in front of a woman. Maybe you and Bull need to retire early like a bunch of old hags and leave the loot for the real men—"

Cobra never got to finish his sentence before Shorty pulled out his gun and planted a bullet in his chest.

Charlotte was accustomed to gunfire and violence, but there was a limit. The look of shock that had been on Cobra's face would forever be etched in her memory. His death should have brought her comfort or peace of mind, but it only made her feel sick. If Shorty was willing to kill someone he had known for years—someone he had been loyal to— then the odds of Charlotte walking away unharmed were slim to none.

Bull dragged Cobra's body outside into the cold so it didn't stink up the cabin. Charlotte grabbed the bottle of whiskey and downed its contents before wiping the back of her hand across her mouth. The alcohol helped to numb her nerves, but it did not replace the fear in her heart.

Chapter 8

It had been two weeks of riding the trains that carried payrolls, hoping to run into Shorty and his gang. Nothing. It was as though they had vanished into thin air and never returned. But Cully had a feeling their efforts weren't the issue.

They were led to believe that someone had been feeding Shorty information from the inside, but it obviously had not been Charlotte, as he originally suspected. Cully received news from New Mexico that Charlotte Dean's story checked out.

His band of hired guns were getting tired of chasing ghosts, and he didn't blame them. Cully himself was getting pretty irritated running into dead ends at every turn. Shorty was good at covering his tracks, but he wasn't that good. Everyone left a trail of some kind.

The gang must have been on the move each time Cully and his crew was aboard the trains. An informant was the only thing that made sense, given how long Charlotte herself had been hunting them down with nothing to show for it. He wanted answers.

Cully walked right into the Denver & Rio Grande Railway building in Denver. The young lady named Kara was working behind the desk, but this time she seemed nervous.

"Mornin', Kara," he said in greeting.

She looked around anxiously but smiled politely. "Good morning, Mr. McCullough. What can I do for you?"

Cully noticed a rather expensive diamond bracelet on the girl's wrist. It was something well above the pay grade of an office assistant, even one who worked for a railway company. He shook his head. "I'm just waitin' to see Mr. Jackson. How've you been these past weeks?"

"Good, Mr. McCullough. I'm heading out of state soon to stay with some family up north, so I don't know if I'll be here next time you visit."

Yeah, she looked about ready to run.

Not the usual behavior of a person with a clean conscience. Cully moved closer, crowding her space but nothing more. His sheer size was enough to intimidate hardened criminals, so Kara shouldn't be much different. She wasn't. He felt like a heel when she started to cry, but he needed information.

"I ain't gonna hurt you, Kara. I just need to know what you've been tellin' Shorty and when the next train will be hit. Please, people died durin' their last raid. I need to know."

"My name is Valerie. I've worked for Shorty since he kidnapped me. I was a fool to think he loved me," she cried out.

The situation was more complicated than he had thought. Shorty had manipulated this young woman and used her affections to fulfill his own cruel agenda. "Valerie, I know he gave you the money for that bracelet. I ain't gonna turn you in, but I need you to tell me what he knows."

"Tomorrow. The biggest payroll of the year will be moved on tomorrow morning. The train leaves Denver and will be headed toward a different camp for the workers. I would tell you were the hideout is, but he'll be gone by the time you find it... Shorty is gonna kill me when he finds out."

The young woman was a blubbering mess of emotions, but he was sympathetic toward her. She had been a victim in all of Shorty's games. He helped her gather her things and instructed her to just head out of town as soon as possible.

Cully sauntered directly into William S. Jackson's office and ripped up his contract. "We won't be on the next train. I'll be out-of-town tonight and so will my men. I would advise you not to hire any more contractors, just don't get involved. Shorty and his guys ain't been hittin' your trains in weeks. It's over, but I don't want the money because he ain't been captured."

It was a front, of course. There would be souls making snow angels in Hell before he gave up. Thankfully his excuse was believed despite the fact that he was a terrible actor, so he walked down to the bar where Mateo and the others waited. They had all grown close over the past weeks despite their differences and constant failures. But now they had a real lead, one that came directly from the source of their problems.

Wolf looked up at him and said, "I haven't seen you smile in what feels like forever, my friend."

"How many times must I tell you that he is not angry or bitter—that is just his face," Mateo quipped.

Cully made a rude gesture that caused the group to burst into laughter, but he sat down beside them. Cully released a heavy sigh. "Kara—or Valerie—the president of the DRGW's assistant was the one leakin' information to Shorty. She's headed out-of-town now for her own protection, but she let it slip that they're hittin' the westbound train leavin' tomorrow morning. Jackson thinks we're headin' out of Denver as we speak, but we'll be on that train. And we'll get this job done if it's the last thing I do."

"New Year's Day?" Wolf asked with a scowl that was an appropriate representation of the animal he was named after.

Mateo let out a long whistle. "There will be a lot of passengers on that train. Many of them will be families traveling home after the holidays. We will either have to evacuate them into another car before the gang arrives or be ready to take them on outside without cover. Either way, not everyone will be walking away from this fight."

"Yeah, but the loss won't be on our end for once," Wolf said. "I think we should stick to Cully's plan this time. We disguise ourselves in case his men come aboard, then we use the element of surprise to our advantage."

Cully nodded his head and then stated, "We need to make sure people don't panic. Last time, we informed the passengers of what was happenin' in hopes that it would work, but we were wrong. This time, no one will know we're on board. The gang will most likely use a very unexpected way of stoppin' the train, so when it happens, Dani and James will escort the passengers in the front rows into the dining car, while Mateo and I meet them head-on. We're outnumbered only by one, so we shouldn't have a hard time of it."

"Shorty usually stays behind until the shooting stops," Wolf mentioned. "What if we attack and he makes a run for it?"

"I'll handle Shorty. Just focus on keepin' the passengers safe from the gunfire." Cully sat down at the small table beside the window. He finished his dinner as he stared out at the storm raging outside. White, furious blankets of snow blew through Denver.

———

Shorty peered into the fire. The smoldering embers reflected in his eyes, unaffected by the ice in his gaze. Charlotte had fallen asleep on the floor in front of the fire in an attempt to stay warm during the storm.

Time and time again, she turned down his offer to join his gang—all the while she had been cozying up to him for her own safety. Charlotte Dean was intelligent, with the instincts of a seasoned hunter, but her youthful appearance was still startling. It caused men to underestimate her, but Shorty was not one of those men. He knew firsthand how dangerous a woman could be, especially when they were forced into a corner. "Wake up, girl."

She stirred, tossing a pillow at him before burying her head under the pillow.

He almost smiled, but instead he walked over and stole the blanket from her. "Are you wanting me to shoot you? Because I will and I'll use your hide to keep warm."

He chuckled quietly to himself. Miss Charlotte Dean was charming and would be a lovely addition to his gang. She almost reminded him of his baby sister, rest her soul.

"Git on up, Charlotte. I need to plan for the next raid, and I can't do that with you snorin' the entire time," he scolded.

"A lady never snores."

"Good thing you ain't no lady, then." Shorty walked into the small kitchen and lit a fire in the oven. He wanted to reheat one of Valerie's pies because no one at the cabin could cook to save their lives—including Charlotte. And another plate of Mad-Dog's gruel was sure to rip a hole in his stomach.

"You ain't going to wish me a happy new year or anything?" Charlotte joked. "What's the plan?"

"Usually there're fireworks and whatever else them stuff-suits up in New York do around this time of year." Shorty stood by the stove, impatiently tapping his foot, uncomfortable under Charlotte's questioning. He shuffled and fidgeted with the end of his shirt.

Charlotte quirked a brow at him, not amused by his hedging. "I was talking about with the raid, not them boys back east. Answer the question."

"We mask up and head to the gorge. Set fire to the trestle to stop the train. We move in from there. Goin' in with our pistols drawn and our heads on straight," he replied. "You're stayin' behind with Bull while the rest of us ride out. We're only after the money this time."

"You expect me to believe you ain't killing nobody when you get there? Come on, Shorty. Give me more credit than that."

"It ain't the goal, all right?" he disclosed. "It's just what happens when things go wrong."

"What about all the other times when Mad-Dog, Cobra, or Jessie killed in cold blood? You telling me you had nothing to do with that? Is this the part where you try to convince me that you're the outlaw with a heart?"

"No. I ain't got a heart. Cut that burden out a long time ago. To be honest, I've been numb to the world for years. In some ways, I think I'm exactly what Cully fears will happen to him one of these days."

Charlotte looked confused, so he explained himself.

"I had a similar upbringin' as Cully way back when. Cut from the same cloth in some ways. Orphaned out of the blue and left to the rest of the world to be shaped by violence. We just ended up on opposite sides of the law." He could tell his confession stunned her. "He'll either turn or end it all."

"Which is why you know so much about the sins committed by the son of a preacher," she observed. "And why you let him live on the train."

"Our paths will cross again, and Cully will have to make a choice on who he really is. If he's been chasin' us to bring us to justice, then he's the avengin' angel he's rumored to be. But if he's after revenge... That's all it takes to send a man to the other side." The smell of warm pie filled the kitchen, distracting Shorty from the conversation. He removed the pie carefully and sat down to eat.

Charlotte wouldn't let him drop it entirely though. "Men," she huffed. "Y'all are always thinking you know what's best for everybody else. Meanwhile, you're blinded by your own foolishness to see what's actually going on."

"And you can see it?" Shorty was skeptical but willing to hear her out. There wasn't much else for him to do, anyway.

"Of course," Charlotte stated matter-of-factly. "This wouldn't be the first time Cully was out for revenge. His entire career has been based on vengeance. The difference between you and Cully is that he didn't let it consume him."

Considering that Shorty's men had been dodging Cully for the past few weeks, he didn't think Charlotte was completely correct in her assumptions. No, there was a part of Cully that thrived in darkness, a part of Cully that Shorty wanted to see alive and kicking before he killed the bounty hunter. "It hasn't consumed him yet, but one day it will."

Chapter 9

After the blizzard settled, a new storm blew through the west. Shorty sat perched in his saddle, peering out over the jagged cliffs of the Royal Gorge. He waited for his gang to arrive. They had no idea the risk they were heading into.

The location alone would add an unsettling amount of danger to their plan. One false move and everything had the potential to end in a gory mess. Bull arrived first. "How are we gonna do this, Louis? There ain't no way we can raid the train if it makes it up to the bridge."

"That's why we're settin' it on fire so they have to stop at the bottom of the gorge. Right where we want them. We stick to the plan and make sure we have a way out. No matter what, we all make it out alive. Ain't no use in robbin' all these trains if we can't spend the loot." Shorty pulled his jacket tighter against the cold wind. "You ain't ridin' this time, anyway. I need you to sit with Charlotte."

"This wouldn't be your way of keepin' me outta the line of fire so Mary don't get upset, would it?"

"I need someone to make sure she don't run off... but yeah, that too. I'm the only reason you're in this life to begin with, and I won't be the reason it ends." Shorty coughed badly.

The air on top of the ledge was thin and colder than it had been when he rode near the bottom of the gorge to scope the area as always. Mad-Dog, Jessie, Whip, and Trapper joined them a little while later. They looked tired and weary. Trapper had the look of a man wanting to do something stupid.

"What's your problem?" Shorty asked.

"You shot Cobra, and we're supposed to follow you still?"

"I ain't forcin' you to do this job, boys. Y'all can cut tail and run like a bunch of cowards. You're here to get paid and stay alive. If you want to follow him to the grave... keep runnin' at the mouth like you are now," he threatened.

They didn't have the guts to question him—either that or they're hurting for the cash. While Shorty and Bull were fond of stashing their earnings, the rest of the gang wasn't so responsible with the money they made. He never understood the urge to spend money on things that weren't necessary for survival. Even though he loved the money that came from robbing trains, Shorty just wanted to live comfortably. The rest was just for sport.

The rest of the gang moved into position while Jessie climbed the trestle to set it on fire. The sun started to shine through the trees and wash the beautiful but deadly landscape in an eerie glow. Bull clucked his tongue and headed back to Independence Pass, using the shortcut path that led directly to their hideout.

Shorty had shown his gang the hidden roads and trails throughout the mountains of Colorado. Without them, it would take hours or up to several days to travel where they needed to go. The trails were dangerous, overgrown, and in prime hunting locations for the remaining tribes in the area, as well as wild animals. Which was worse, he couldn't tell anymore.

He joined Trapper, Whip, and Mad-Dog at the bottom of the gorge. The valley was calm and serene with the streams frozen over and the area all but abandoned during the troubled winters. Most folks would freeze to death out in the cold no matter how prepared they thought they were.

Whip struck a match and lit the end of a cigar.

"Celebratin' early?" Shorty asked.

"Nope. Just enjoyin' myself in case we don't make it out of here in one piece. I'm quite fond of all of my pieces."

"We'll make it out. Valerie's last letter before she left said that Cully and his men headed to Fort Collins. Said he ended his contract with the railway president and took off." Shorty knew Valerie was true to her word. She had worked for him with complete loyalty and admiration on her part.

As much as he would have liked to send her up north in payment of her services as he had promised, Shorty had sent an anonymous telegram to a sheriff in Boulder, Colorado where she was set to board her train.

Valerie would be detained and sent to trial for stealing confidential company information and aiding a known criminal in a conspiracy to commit a robbery. Whatever other charges they decided to arrest her for, he wasn't sure and he didn't care. By the time everything was said and done, he would be the last man standing.

Making a clean getaway was all that mattered after the robbery was completed. They couldn't afford to have someone on the outside with information regarding the locations of their safe houses or the intricacies of their operation. Valerie knowing their identities, alone, made her a liability he could not afford. She would hate him, but he was comfortable with that.

Nothing could go unchecked.

"Get into position. The train will be arrivin' within the hour. This is a dangerous area, so watch yourselves."

Shorty whistled loud enough for it to echo against the tall walls of rock in the Royal Gorge. Jessie heard his signal and lit the fires that would block the train from passing and force it to stop. The cold wind made it difficult for the fire to catch at first, but Jessie worked it into a full blaze. Down the line, they could hear the rattling sounds of the train approaching.

Jessie climbed on his horse and traveled back down the path toward them. Excitement warred with the trepidation he felt, causing a nauseating bubble to form in his gut. Instinct told him to sit this one out, but pride made him stay put.

The train came around the bend at high speeds before the break was engaged and brought the train to a screeching halt. A smile curled on Shorty's leathery face that was reddened by the cold mountain winds. Trapper, Mad-Dog, Jessie, and Whip made their way toward the train. Their movements were quiet and quick, using the environment to their advantage as they infiltrated the train. He crept closer to the attack sight and waited for the signal, his hands gripping the reins and his hat pulled low.

Shorty thought back to the day he had nearly lost his life. He had been pinned down by gunfire, fighting for the dream of another outlaw who lived by no code at all. An outlaw without honor was simply a criminal or a madman. He watched each member of the gang get gunned down by Cully and the other bounty hunters on the contract. For a split second, he had made the decision to run instead of submitting to the authorities. The sound of a rifle going off echoed in his ears just before fire exploded against his back.

The last he had seen was the face of Cully McCullough.

Charlotte Dean redressed into the clothes they had abducted her in. Her boots were laced tightly, and her hair was tucked beneath her hat as always. Her heart pounded against her chest. It was as simple as opening the door and walking past the threshold, but for some reason, Charlotte wasn't moving as quickly as she should.

No, her time with Shorty hadn't changed her mind. She was too smart for this sort of mind game, but something had made her want to stay and see how everything played out. Charlotte wanted to see him dead for the death of her friend. But at the same time, Shorty had been correct about a few things. There was no way of denying his perceptiveness.

The front door opened right when she removed her jacket. Bull walked in. In most ways, he was the beating heart of the gang. So different from when she had first met him, Bull had settled down and gained a sense of reason. And he was her only chance of making it out alive again. Sure, she could take that leap like before, and Bull might just let her go... but there was still the risk of Shorty doing to her what he had done to Valerie.

"I need your help," Charlotte said quietly. The big man before her removed his hat and sat down in a chair to listen. "I turned him away too many times. There ain't no reason to keep me around anymore. No more games to play."

Bull's voice was all smoke and gravel as he spoke, resonating a deep baritone rumble with every word. "Louis won't let you go. He don't let anybody go... only me. He said he wanted everybody out alive just so they would go through with the job. It's gotten so bad, he's lyin' to himself. But I know him, and if things go wrong, he ain't stayin' behind to save nobody."

"You think something is going to happen?"

"I know it is. And Louis should know better than to think Cully would walk away from this so easily. Not a man worth his salt would leave his pride beaten down in such a way," Bull said before he coughed into the sleeve of his jacket. "I told him before the train robberies started up again that his luck would run dry because of Cully."

"I think you're right, but isn't there a part of you that wants him to get caught?" Charlotte's eyes searched the face of Shorty's best friend. "Maybe facing the reality of his crimes is what he needs."

"But everythin' he's done, he's done for a reason."

"Do those reasons justify the people who have lost their lives or their incomes because of him? Listen to yourself, Bull. Think about the miners who ain't getting paid or the children that survive the raids who are forced to live with the memory of being held at gunpoint," Charlotte pleaded.

"What do you want me to do? Turn in my best friend or leave him high and dry like everybody else in his life?"

"I'm asking that you take responsibility for your actions and make sure the others do the same. You have to know that this ain't gonna end well for all of you if Cully really is aboard that train." Charlotte walked over to Bull and placed her hand on his shoulder. He looked up at her with watery eyes and crumpled in his seat. "Go to the stash houses and get the money. If you turn it over to the authorities, they might be more lenient with you."

"How do you know?"

"Because Cully would force them to. He believes in redemption and that a man can make the decision to change."

Bull seemed to consider her offer. She wasn't sure if he had it in him to betray the only person he had ever been loyal to besides his wife, but she had faith that he would at least try to change the situation. Bull wasn't a complete barbarian like some other members of the gang.

"If you don't do it for yourself or for Shorty, do it for Mary. She deserves to love a man with a conscience—a man who knows that when things are wrong, he has the strength and will to make them right again." Charlotte took a seat beside Bull and fell into a grim silence.

Whatever decision he chose to make, she would be ready to either fight him or back him up. Charlotte Dean stopped defining her life by the death of her friend and what had happened to her the first time she had been taken hostage.

She no longer viewed herself as a victim.

Charlotte Dean was a survivor, and no matter what the next few hours or days or weeks would bring, she was determined to end Shorty's reign as the most infamous train robber in Colorado.

Chapter 10

When the train came to a full stop, Cully peered out a clouded glass window in the passenger car. The bridge was on fire, which meant they could not pass completely through the gorge unless it was extinguished. It was an ambush.

The information Valerie had given him had paid off. He sprang into action once he spotted two of Shorty's men making their way toward the train. Cully began signaling for the passengers to be escorted to the other cars while he and Mateo readied their rifles. The gang drew closer.

So far, no one on the train had panicked. The travelers moved obediently into the dining car. Cully posted himself at the main entrance, Mateo taking the other. They were quiet, painstakingly waiting for the gang to attempt to ascend upon the train. Mad-Dog and Trapper boarded first, guns drawn, and were greeted by a volley of gunfire.

Outlaws slumped dead against the seats, staining the already red upholstery with the deep shade of blood. The gunfire hadn't alerted Shorty that something had gone amiss until Wolf hit Jesse Elliott and Whip from a few feet beyond a cluster of trees. Cobra didn't appear to be among the gang so that only left Bull and Shorty unaccounted for.

Cully stepped off the train and watched Shorty's escape.

He rushed for the livery car to retrieve Samson, a task that was not so easily accomplished, as the gunshots had startled most of the horses. Mateo followed. Cully strapped the saddle down and secured the saddle bag and the rest of his belongings. Samson was a bit jittery from the cold and the sounds he must have heard while contained in the livery car.

"What are we going to do, señor?"

"Send Dani and James to put out the fire. You and Wolf need to stay with the passengers in case there are more men than we expected. The four of y'all need to escort the train to the last stop." Cully mounted Samson and sheathed his rifle. "I'm huntin' down Shorty, and hopefully I'll find Charlotte Dean along the way. Keep your eyes open, Mateo."

The other man nodded his head before rushing to follow Cully's orders. No passengers had been injured, the money stayed in the possession of the railway, and Cully's entire group of hired guns were still alive. He could walk away and consider it a success, but there was a bit of unfinished business between himself and Shorty. Clearly the outlaw had a crooked sense of honor and an even worse opinion of Cully.

He eased Samson along the uneven, terrain of the Royal Gorge. The wind cut straight through the layers of clothing Cully wore. His teeth clattered so much that he was forced to clench his jaw to stop the sound from rolling around his skull. The air burned his nostrils as the wind nearly blew his hat off his head.

Wind blew the snow around, making him nervous that the trail wouldn't be as easy to follow as he originally thought. If the snow covered up the tracks leading to wherever Shorty had escaped to, Cully would be stuck out in the cold for days.

With Samson, he took off in the direction Shorty had gone in. There were slight traces of broken twigs and rustled leaves that gave an indication to the path the outlaw had taken. Cully pulled out a map from the lapels of his jacket. The trail he was on didn't appear in the area. Not that a lot of folk would be out in the gorge anyway, but it was still peculiar.

Samson whinnied as the smoke from the fire on the trestle blackened the sky. The smell of soot and ash mingled in the air, tainting the fresh scent of the newly fallen snow. Part of Cully regretted shooting the outlaws instead of taking them in, but he and Mateo would have been outnumbered in the passenger car if they hadn't. And he owed Mateo and his family too much to have allowed him to die by the hands of some morally impaired outlaws they were after.

Cully traveled for six miles, unable to find anything out of the ordinary. The trail had gone cold—both figuratively and literally—and the wind had started to pick up speed. Cully pulled Samson into a cave that sat near the edge of the gorge to wait out the storm that had been brewing. He pulled what paper he had with him out of the saddlebags to use as kindling.

He refused to burn Maria's letters.

The thought of her being out there alone and possibly in danger didn't sit right with him at all. She was a dear friend, and she deserved far more than what the West had to offer. La Rosa being burned to the ground was probably some sort of racial attack most likely, but Cully knew the sort of men

Maria offered sanctuary to. Heck, she had put him up for ages without so much as a dime in return.

Of course he had offered to pay for the room, but she had insisted that he and Wesley had become like family. And to Maria nothing was more sacred than her *familia*.

A branch snapped to the left, slightly startling Samson. Cully chose to pretend like he didn't hear it while he dug for his gun. Instead of snow, rain began to fall from the sky in a half-frozen assault on the land. He poked at the small fire before lifting his rifle. Two men appeared from the shadows.

Mateo and Wolf.

Cully cursed beneath his breath and set his rifle on the ground beside him. The smiles on their faces were smug and annoying to say the least. "I could have shot y'all."

Wolf snorted. "If we wanted to sneak up on you, we wouldn't have made so much noise. You wouldn't have seen us coming if we wished you harm, my friend."

Cully didn't argue that. He didn't know Wolf's skills entirely, and Mateo was very secretive about where he had been for several months. The two men were every bit of an enigma as he was. "I thought I told you two to escort the train to Aspen. What made you come back?"

"Dani and James had it covered. Besides, we came to find you because you still have not paid us for the job, señor," Mateo said, earning himself a punch to the shoulder from Wolf.

"What this fool is trying to say is that we came to help you track down Shorty and cover your back in case things blow up in your face again." It was Wolf's turn to get punched, but the punch came from Cully instead of Mateo.

"I had to stop for the night. I couldn't let Samson get sick huntin' this lowlife down. He ain't worth the dirt off my boots let alone the life of my horse," Cully explained. "But we'll head out once it stops again. Shouldn't be too hard to find Shorty. He ain't exactly the most subtle outlaw I've tracked down."

Shorty was confused. Never before had he heard of Cully shooting a man before the crime had been committed. Sure, his men had deserved it, probably more than the bounty hunter was aware. But after watching the back of Mad-Dog's head get blown off before he could take more than two steps through the entrance of the passenger car, he had been stunned.

That cold-blooded side of Cully McCullough had started to rear its ugly head, and Shorty wasn't sure the bounty hunter was even aware of it.

Freezing cold rain dripped down the back of his coat. Shorty's hair was wet and matted to his face. His breath came out in puffs of smoke as the tremors set in. He was sure to catch a fever way out in the middle of nowhere. Luckily, the new safe house was only a few miles north from where he was.

It wasn't uncommon for it to rain in the dead of winter, especially in the mountains where the weather was usually unpredictable. The drop in temperature was the dangerous part, especially if a rider's clothing had been soaked through.

Shorty's hands grew stiff, his body chilled to the bone. He knew his horse had been struggling with the cold as well, but he couldn't waste time by setting camp. He pushed hard and forward until the flickering lights from the safe house caught his attention. Shorty nearly collapsed off the side of his saddle when he arrived, but luckily Charlotte Dean has seen him ride up the mountain.

He could barely comprehend anything beside the heat of her palms when she cupped his cheeks in her hands. Bull came out of the cabin a few moments later to tend to the horse while Charlotte helped him inside.

She led him over to the fireplace. "What happened? You weren't supposed to be back for another six hours!" she shouted as she removed his coat and the layers of wet clothing from his body.

"You ain't goin' to wish me a happy new year or anything?" Shorty mocked, using Charlotte's words from before. She slapped him across the face, but he didn't care because he could barely feel it. His skin was numb. "Cully was on the train. He killed the others, and I made a run for it."

"Did you get the money?" Bull asked from the doorway.

"We didn't get that far before they started shootin'. The men he brought looked like normal folk, so we didn't assume anythin'. Opened fire as soon as the boys boarded the train."

Charlotte looked at him as though he disgusted her. And he should. Why would he expect anything else in her eyes? "What are we doing next, Shorty?"

"We head to Independence Pass after the weather changes. Then Bull will gather the money, while you and I come up with a plan on how to git out of town before Cully finds us," he whispered between shuddered breaths. "You didn't think I was gonna leave you behind, did you?"

"What use do you have for me anymore? Why not just run for the border so they can't catch you?" Charlotte moved away from him to grab a bottle of whiskey he assumed she had been drinking before he arrived. She took a big gulp before she continued, "If you promise me an equal cut of the loot you've saved up, I'll help you. But no more locking me up or leaving me behind when you leave. I see everything or I do nothing."

For a moment, Shorty couldn't believe the words Charlotte had said. He wasn't sure if he had the courage to trust his own hearing after everything that had happened that day.

———————

Charlotte saw him take the bait, again. If she could buy Cully time by sabotaging Shorty, it would increase her chances of survival. She would never do anything outwardly illegal, it just wasn't her character. However, Shorty had put her into a position where she didn't have much of a choice.

"I only have three rules, Shorty. Number one, I don't kill unless it is to defend myself. Number two, I ain't nobody's lackey. I'm equal, or I ain't nothing, got it? Number three, don't try to play mind games with me. I ain't easy to manipulate, and I'll prove you wrong time and time again."

Shorty started to flex his fingers by the fire. He simply nodded his head and looked at Charlotte over his shoulder. Something in his eyes had changed. The confidence that had once been there was gone. Cully's actions had shaken

Shorty's reality off balance. Charlotte wasn't sure if that was an advantage she could exploit or something that was dangerous for everyone involved.

A clear-headed, rational Shorty was hard to predict, but if he had nothing left to lose... no one was safe.

Charlotte walked toward him with cautious steps. She knelt beside him and wrapped a blanked around his shoulders before offering him some liquor. He accepted both but turned back to stare into the flames. She looked up at Bull who had been looking over them.

Concern was etched into his expression. "You gonna be all right, Louis?" the big man asked.

Shorty nodded his head again but remained quiet. His silence hovered in the air like a bad omen.

Chapter 11

The rain had stopped after sunrise the next morning. Cully lifted his weary bones from the bedroll beside the fire and packed up camp. Mateo snored loudly near the back of the small cave until Cully kicked his boots to wake him up, dodging the pillow that came flying at his head in the process.

Wolf had been on the trail before sunrise. The man was so eager to find Charlotte that Cully had started to suspect that he harbored feelings for the female mercenary in the group. He would never confront Wolf about his more personal motivations behind tracking down Shorty. It wasn't in his place to do so.

Mateo finally got up off the ground and went to check on the horses while Cully tended to the camp.

Wolf returned, looking like he hadn't slept at all the night before. He walked over to Cully and said, "There wasn't much to find, but the strange path you found leads up into the mountains. I followed it for a few miles. He definitely went in that direction."

"Thanks for scoutin' ahead, did you find any signs that he met up with anybody else along the way?" Cully wanted to know what they were headed into. "No footprints or nothin' clustered in certain areas? Perhaps the remnants of a camp?"

"No, the trail goes cold about two miles past the initial trail. There was one set of tracks headed in that direction, but it doesn't mean that they don't lead into an ambush, my friend."

Cully understood the man's cautious nature. Mateo joined them again with more news. "I've hunted in the area, so I am familiar with the land. There is a cabin not far from where you are describing. It was abandoned when I found it a few months back. It might not be at this time of the year."

"Charlotte had said they the gang didn't behave like normal outlaws, right?" Cully asked to no one in particular. "What if they live like regular folks between jobs, which is why they take so many precautions to hide their identities?"

"You think they would hide in a regular cabin? Isn't that a bit loco?" Mateo scowled at him in confusion.

"If they didn't want to be found, the best place to hide would be in plain sight. Or in this case, a cabin in the mountains," Wolf clarified before handing Cully his flask. "It will put some fire in your belly for the cold ride up the mountain. You may need it."

Cully accepted the flask and took a swig. He didn't want much though. He liked to keep his mind sharp and his aim steady.

With everyone in agreement, they headed up the mountain following the hidden path that was just barely there. A secret passage through the harsh terrain would be a great advantage to a criminal like Louis Gerhard. Wolf led them to where his trail ended, and then Mateo took the lead. He navigated through the forest as though he were native to the area, which told Cully that Mateo liked to live off the land.

Wolf seemed a little off, so Cully pinned him with his infamous *spill your guts* expression and said, "Fork up the goods, Wolf. What's got you distracted?"

"Charlotte," he answered. Cully should have expected as much. "I don't like the thought of her being caught in the middle of this showdown we're bound to run into."

"I don't like it, either. But we have to get her back somehow. Better now than later down the road when she's either traumatized or..."

Wolf cut his eyes at Cully, silently daring him to insinuate that Charlotte would ever turn to Shorty's side. Cully raised his hands in surrender and withheld his judgment. "Charlotte put herself in danger to help all of us, my friend. She would not throw away her pride for something as meaningless as money."

"Maybe you're right, I'm sorry for thinkin' the worst of her. The two of us owe her our lives, and that's a debt I intend to pay back in full." Cully tipped his hat to his friend and turned toward Mateo next.

Of course, Mateo shot him a mischievous smile that warned Cully that the man would most likely deflect his questions with ill-timed humor.

Either way, Cully still wanted to ask. "You've been huntin' in these parts, but you've never come across Shorty and his crew?"

"Señor, most of the cabins up here were destroyed a long time ago. I didn't even expect to find one left standing. It was back before I showed up for Grace and Wesley's wedding. The cabin had been cleaned spotless and abandoned for all I knew."

"Did you steal anythin'?"

Mateo clutched his heart in mock horror. "I am offended, señor. Besides, why confess my crimes to a bounty hunter?"

"You would be surprised how many times I've heard that same line from outlaws over the years, Mateo. And with Maria missin' I would think you would be more forthcomin' with your information," Cully said pointedly.

"What are you saying?"

"I'm sayin' you're suspect number one for motives somebody would have to want to kidnap your sister. Seein' as I ain't got a clue about what you've been up to, for all I know it has somethin' to do with that."

Mateo stopped his horse and turned around to look Cully in his eyes. "I got a letter from a woman saying that she gave birth to my son two years ago."

"You left to track him down?" Cully asked.

"I found where he had been living. Stayed in the house for a few weeks, hoping they would come back, but they never did. Been searching for him ever since, living off the land because I have no money for food or shelter." Mateo turned back around and pushed on toward the cabin. "When there was no trace of them, I went home to La Rosa."

"Why keep it a secret?"

"Because I felt shame and anger for being exactly like my own father. I was not there for my son, and I should have been."

Cully shook his head. "She didn't tell you about your son, Mateo. How could you have known? It ain't your fault."

"What would you have me feel guilty for then? Do you want me to be angry about being absent in my child's life or blame myself for Maria's disappearance? Because I've been doing a lot of both lately." Mateo rushed ahead of them.

Earlier that morning, Charlotte gathered her things while Shorty and Bull readied the horses. Bull's horse carried his share of the money, Shorty's horse carried his, and Charlotte got her own loot.

The three of them had split what remained of the other men's small fortunes into equal parts. She was a bit disappointed that Bull decided to remain loyal to Shorty after their discussion.

There had to be a way to leave a clue behind for Cully and the others. *Think, Charlotte! Think!*

Inspiration struck, and she searched around to make sure she hadn't been watched. Charlotte carved the words *INDEPENDENCE PASS* into the wall beside the bed in the room she had slept in. Just when she had moved the mattress back into place, Shorty knocked on the door.

"One second," Charlotte called out. A few moments later she emerged from the room and followed him out to where the horses waited. It was strange not seeing the others, but Charlotte kept quiet until they were off toward their destination. "So we come up with the plan to leave once we get back to Independence Pass?"

Shorty, who had finally regained some sense, spoke up. "It's the only place I feel secure after what happened.

Besides, all of our legal documents are there that need to be destroyed."

"If I die or get taken down, I want to die as myself. No need to hide who I really am or leave the responsibility of my actions unclaimed," Charlotte responded.

The two men paused for a moment.

"You ain't been on this side of the law for long, so you wouldn't exactly understand why takin' a name is important."

"No, but I've worked as a mercenary long enough to know that my hands ain't clean just because it's what I like to tell myself before I lay down my head at night." Her words coaxed out one of Shorty's rare smiles. "If y'all keep hanging on to that mentality that it ain't a crime until you get caught, then the crime is going to end up getting you shot not captured."

"I've been shot enough times to know it's survivable. Goin' to trial will most likely end up with me swingin' by my neck somewhere. And I ain't too eager to meet that end just yet." Shorty's smile never faltered as he spoke.

Charlotte looked to the other man that rode with them. "What are your plans after all of this, Bull?"

"Thought I'd take Mary down to Mexico and stay there for a little while, maybe for good if we like it," that gruff voice admitted. "She's fond of the ocean, so I think she will."

"I'm thinkin' bout headin' up north to Canada. Heard it ain't much different from these mountains here. I ain't the sort to do well in the warm weather. I've always been drawn to the cold, untamed lands of these parts."

In a way, Charlotte thought her question was a bit cruel, considering that Bull and Shorty would likely be captured by Cully. But their confessions had piqued her interests. It was strange to think that these outlaws had dreams of their own.

Most men turned to crime for fame and reputation or money and other forms of personal gain but not them. Perhaps for Shorty, the fun and games he had planned were at an end.

Charlotte thought for a moment about her own dream. She imagined herself tucked away in the woods with the mercenary life behind her. At only twenty-two years old, she had plenty of time to find a nice man and raise a few children. Charlotte had always wanted to be a mother. But she could only imagine herself spending the rest of her life with one man—her best friend and partner in crime: Wolf.

"What's got you all pink in the cheeks?" Shorty asked suspiciously. "Ain't never seen that look on your face before. It's the look of a woman fancyin' after a man."

"I guess he has always been there, I just never truly realized how important he was. But now that I'm more than likely riding to my own death, I'm sad that I won't get to see him one last time. Or hear his voice."

"What's your fondest memory of him? Thinkin' bout it might keep your mind off of things," Bull suggested. "And it might provide some much-needed entertainment for the ride."

She hesitated for a moment, but seeing as they shared when they could have ignored her questions, Charlotte decided to answer sincerely.

"We were in a bar trying to hustle a few crooks in a game of poker, but we kept playing each other even after everybody left. Wolf and I had been riding together for years, but for the first time—with the drinks flowing and the game distracting us—we bared our souls to one another." She smiled fondly. "That was until he tried to cheat and steal my cut. So I bit him hard on his arm. Hasn't shut up about it since."

"You sure know the way into a man's heart, Miss Charlotte Dean. Explains why you nearly cleaned us out in a simple game of Black Jack," Shorty accused. "Could have warned us, you know?"

Chapter 12

Cully, Wolf, and Mateo pulled their horses around to the back of the cabin in case Shorty and his men were still inside. Cully approached from the right, and Wolf approached from the left, while Mateo tied up the horses. No sounds came through the windows, but that didn't mean anything.

Cully and Wolf kicked in the front door to find nobody home. The cabin had been cleaned thoroughly and organized like a display in one of those fancy furniture shops back east. Not even a book was out of place. Mateo joined them, throwing his hands up in the air in frustration.

"How long ago did they leave?" Mateo asked.

Wolf shook his head. Cully began to search the place.

Charlotte had been right again. The cabin wasn't the usual hideout for a gang of outlaws. No maps pinned to the wall, no ammunition boxes, no boarded windows, or the remnants of a card game on the table. Even the liquor bottles were organized in a neat, orderly fashion. "Check the bedrooms," Cully instructed. He walked over to the fireplace. A bit of heat radiated off the ashes. "We can't be more than five hours behind them. Catchin' up should be easy unless they take another hidden path through the mountains."

"All the bedrooms are clear, even the beds were made," Mateo shouted from the other room. "What about you, Wolf?"

"Charlotte left us a little message, my friends."

Cully and Mateo walked into the bedroom where Wolf had been searching for signs of the gang's whereabouts. He pushed the bed away from the wall a few inches. Carved into the wall were the words *INDEPENDENCE PASS* in big, bold letters. Wolf had been right. Charlotte Dean wanted Shorty behind bars just as much as they did.

"If we head out now, we may be able to catch them before they reach the pass. Dependin' on which way they went and how fast we ride," Cully said.

The three men rushed back to their horses so fast Cully felt like he had been running in a footrace. He took off in the direction of Aspen. The gang's safe house couldn't be too far from the first payroll train attack he had been on board for. Shorty seemed to know more about the Colorado wilderness than most rangers or hunters that were local to the area.

It took them several days to get to Aspen from the Royal Gorge, which meant the trail had gone cold. Cully asked around town if the folks knew of any cabins up in the mountains, especially ones that were well taken care of. According to a few miners in town, there were three in total that hadn't been purchased by the railway or the mining companies. Cully wanted to check all three.

On the journey there, the weather had been their worst hindrance. A few times, Cully thought Wolf had been on the verge of freezing to death.

Cully walked into the room and tossed masks and other gear at the two men who slept in the beds. They startled awake—guns drawn but harmless in a fatigued state of mind. He shook his head at them. "Get up, put all that on, and meet me by the horses," he instructed.

It took them less than an hour to follow his orders.

"We can't stay here. I know it's cold, and we ain't really had a wink of sleep, but the locals say there are three possible cabins up in these mountains. Which means in order to cover more ground, we need to split up." Cully pulled three maps out of his back pocket and unfolded them while the others readied their mounts. "Wolf, you take the one south from here. Mateo, you go east. And I'll head to the west."

Wolf shook his hand. "Good luck, my friend. But do not do anything foolish until we can cover your back."

"I could say the same to y'all. You boys have a heck of a time followin' my orders, even though I'll be the one handin' out the money when this is over."

Mateo laughed. "It is not that we do not follow your orders. It is that you don't always make sense, and it is very easy to get confused. We either do what you say or read between the lines and do what you need us to do, señor."

"Yeah, I bet." Cully rolled his eyes.

Wolf and Mateo took the maps he offered before climbing into their saddles. The horses had to be just as tired as the men riding them if not more so. Cully patted Samson's side and promised him a big treat when they got home.

What was supposed to be a quick job had turned into another adventure for the duo. He would have to make it up to him, or Samson would turn ornery on the ride back to Durango.

From inside, Charlotte watched Shorty as he rode his horse up the steep incline that led to the cabin. He was furious and ready to shoot something, she could tell by the look in his eyes. And if she didn't know better that something would be Charlotte Dean. He opened the door before he slammed it behind himself. The frame cracked upon the thunderous bang.

Charlotte launched herself across the room and leveled her revolver on him as she pretended that she hadn't been watching. Charlotte cursed and lowered her weapon before she walked over to him. "I could have shot you, Shorty! What the heck were you thinking, bursting in here like that?"

Shorty grabbed Charlotte by her hair and pressed his knife to her throat. She closed her eyes for a moment and then looked him in the eye with more of that foolish courage that seemed to seep through her pores.

"I'm only gonna ask you once, Charlotte. Why is Cully pokin' around Aspen, lookin' for a cabin in Independence Pass? You wouldn't be leadin' him, would you?" Shorty inquired, the threat evident in his biting tone. "If I don't like the answer you have for me, I'll be guttin' you right here."

Charlotte swallowed against the blade. She didn't so much as flinch when it cut her slightly. "I am leading him here. There ain't no way we're getting out of the country or even across state lines with him on our trail. There ain't no way for him to ambush us here. We have the upper hand. Lead him near the fire and burn him ourselves."

"You didn't think to tell me about this little plan of yours?"

Warm blood slowly dripped in a thin line down the pale column of her neck. She tried her best to hide her bluffing. "I knew you would react like this. But it was a risk I was willing to take if it meant we made it out of here in one piece." Charlotte looked over to Bull. "We already know he threatened Valerie before she left for Boulder. Like you said, Cully's got a dark side, and we don't know what he's capable of when he's desperate. What if he goes after Mary?"

Shorty pulled the knife away. His eyes were suspicious, but he didn't question her further.

"How long did it take you to rush up the mountain, Shorty?"

"Two hours. I couldn't use the usual path after nearly runnin' into your little Indian friend."

Charlotte's heart dropped to her toes. If Wolf traveled up the mountain alone, he would be outnumbered and caught unaware. She had to think of something fast, or else she would never live to see her dream become a reality. "Is that so?" she asked as indifferently as she could muster.

"Dang near ran clean into him. He can't be too far away now. Not sure exactly if he'll attack when he finds the cabin or alert the others, but we'll be ready for him." Shorty shot her look. "That won't be a problem for you, will it?"

Charlotte's bravery didn't shake under the scrutiny of his gaze or the harshness of his tone. "I may have feelings for the man, but I ain't stupid. I need this money and betraying you wouldn't be in my best interest."

"Good," he said simply.

She watched as Shorty blacked out the lights and put out the fire. He pulled the curtains open and allowed only the natural light from outside stream in through the windows. Charlotte could see more clearly outside while she stood in the darkness, which meant that Wolf could not see them inside of the cabin. He would never know that Bull and Shorty propped the ends of their rifles on the windowsills.

Just then, Charlotte spotted a blur of movement behind the trees. She knew Shorty and Bull had seen it too, but they held their fire. They waited for Wolf to get into position. Charlotte pretended to load her own rifle and take aim, but she used it to bash Bull over the side of the head.

She could defend herself against Shorty a lot easier than his hulking partner. Shorty elbowed her in the face and knocked the rifle to the floor and attempted to turn his own rifle against her. But Charlotte kicked it out of his hand before he could stand up to his full height and overpower her.

He recovered quickly. Shorty slammed his fist into her stomach, and he reached for the revolver in his side holster. Charlotte rammed her knee into his groin and kicked his knee out from under him. The revolver slid across the hardwood floor. While Shorty struggled to clear the stars behind his eyelids, Charlotte ran for the door. Her only goal was to save Wolf, even at the risk of her own life. Nothing else mattered, only him.

Charlotte opened the front door and inhaled deeply.

Chapter 13

"Run, Wolf!" Charlotte Dean felt the blade plunge into her side only seconds after she screamed her warning. Bull regained consciousness but ignored her to cover Shorty while he opened fire on the man. Wolf just barely avoided a shot to the chest from Bull's rifle. She was held up only by Shorty's arm around her waist and the leverage he had on the knife.

She tasted the blood on her tongue. Charlotte could hear Wolf as he bellowed out her name like a prayer to the gods. She wanted nothing more than to comfort him and soothe the ache in his soul. Shorty finally allowed her to drop like a sack of wet sand to the floor. He casually stepped over her and leveled his rifle at Wolf.

Wolf peeked out from behind the cover of a felled tree and aimed his firearm at Shorty. Charlotte wanted to buy him more time, so she pressed her hand against the gushing wound and scooted herself across the floor.

Charlotte pulled herself behind the wall between the foyer and the kitchen. She picked up the revolver she had knocked out of Shorty's hand and fired it into the air. They turned on her in an instant. The sound of gunfire from behind drew the outlaws' attention to her.

It gave Wolf enough time to get into position or to run for help. She fired wildly from around the corner of the wall.

Charlotte had no desire to shoot anyone, not even Shorty, despite what he had done to her, so she didn't aim the revolver at all. When the gun was empty, she tossed the revolver aside and lifted up one of the rifles that Bull had leaned up against the wall in case they needed the extra firepower.

"Giving up yet, boys?"

"I knew you would turn on me, Charlotte Dean." Shorty belted his words from across the foyer. The room was dark, but she caught his reflection in the mirror that hung on the wall.

"I couldn't let you kill the man I love. Not like that."

"I pity any man who could be loved by a vindictive she-demon like you." He sneered. "I'm prayin' you bleed out on that cold floor. I hope you never see that savage again."

Tears prickled her eyes before they spilled over. "The only savage in these parts is you, Shorty. He's more of an honorable man than you will ever be. You're a coward and a good-for-nothing snake in the grass. I should have shot you when I had the chance."

"Yeah, you should have. Because when I'm done killin' you, I'll be goin' after him—"

"You will die before you can lay a hand on him!" Charlotte's words cut off his little speech. Outlaws talked too much for her liking. She pulled a bottle of liquor off the counter above her head. More blood oozed between her fingers from the effort. She peered around the corner.

Bullets rained down before she could get a good look, but she rolled the bottle across the floor toward them and shot it.

The bottle burst and sent glass flying. She grabbed another to do the same thing. It would do her no good to just shoot blindly and waste all of her bullets when there was plenty of glass to annoy them with.

By the sounds they made, her plan had worked.

She used the mirror to gage their movements and placed skilled shots if they attempted anything. Charlotte had them pinned down for the time being. She only hoped the others showed up in time to help.

"There's a special place beside the Devil for women like you, Charlotte. I hope you meet him soon."

––––––––––––

When Wolf didn't show up at the meeting location, Cully and Mateo traveled south to find him. They followed his tracks several miles up a steep incline that gave way to flat ground. Samson championed the difficult task, but Mateo's horse had not been so lucky. He had been forced to dismount and walk his horse up the side of the mountain safely.

They searched the area after the trail went cold.

Just when they were about to move on to a different location, Wolf ran at them through the trees. His usually tanned face had gone pale, and his legs buckled.

Cully jumped off Samson and went to help the man. "What happened?"

"They set me up, but Charlotte warned me before I could get shot," he said frantically. "Shorty stabbed her. It was bad. He used so much force her feet came off the ground. She distracted them so I could get away. I shouldn't have left her there. What if she—"

Cully placed his hand over Wolf's mouth, cutting him off. They couldn't afford for Wolf to get hysterical. "Calm down, Charlotte needs you right now. I'm gonna go chargin' in to get the heat off of her, but I need y'all to be ready to detain Bull while I distract everyone in the house," Cully ordered

For once, no one argued, cracked jokes, or questioned him. Wolf led them to the cabin. The men took cover, but Cully opened fire as he ran towards the cabin. He waited quietly until he saw Shorty's head appear. *Got you now, Shorty.* Cully took cover beneath the window, confused when he heard a bottle roll across the floor. Seconds later, it exploded into the room.

The outlaws ducked out of the way, but not before Cully caught sight of Charlotte through the mirror. She leaned up against some kitchen storage units with her hand pressed to her side. She didn't look good, but she wasn't dead.

A shotgun cocked. It took out part of the window and wall near where Cully had been hiding. He shook the fragments of wood from his shoulders and looked through what remained of the window once more. Mateo eased through the front door while Wolf laid down cover fire.

Cully watched as the man moved silently. He snuck behind Bull and placed him in a chokehold, dragging the larger man away. When Wolf ran out of ammo, Cully fired into the house to buy him enough time to get to Mateo. Together, the two men tied up Bull and strung him up on the back of one of the outlaws' horses.

Cully reloaded his rifle as Shorty peppered the wall with bullets. He rolled across the shards of glass and snow before charging through the window. A bullet tore through the muscle in his arm, but he managed to tackle Shorty to the ground.

Cully straddled the other man's chest and landed a right hook to his jaw. Shorty spit blood into Cully's face before digging his finger into the wound on Cully's shoulder. When Wolf and Mateo rushed through the door, they couldn't get a clear shot. Cully shouted above the ruckus, "Get Charlotte and Bull out of here, I've got this!"

When Wolf began to protest, Mateo pulled him back and said, "He may be loco, but he has handled a lot worse than this. We really need to get your friend to a doctor."

Cully watched them, his knee planted on Shorty's chest. He needed to make sure his men got out safely before he had his little talk with the outlaw who stood between Cully and a hot bath.

Wolf hesitated only slightly, but eventually rushed to the kitchen and lifted Charlotte into his arms. Wolf followed Mateo back to the horses. He pulled Charlotte onto his lap, using his body heat to keep her warm. She clung to his shoulders as he urged his horse on. Cully had never seen Charlotte so desperate or frightened.

Mateo mounted his own horse and led the poor wind-broken creature that carried Bull safely through the forest. When all four of them were out of sight, Cully moved his weight off of Shorty. "You and I need to have a little discussion, Louis," he said with a thick drawl.

"So now you want to talk? You weren't too eager to talk to my boys before you and that Mexican fella blew their brains all over the gorge. Why now?" Shorty barked challengingly.

Cully limped over to a discarded revolver on the floor. Three bullets were left, which was plenty for what he had planned. He kicked the second revolver over to Shorty who looked at him with wide eyes. Cully clarified, "Your men killed all but two of my hired guns along with several passengers on the last train. They were paid back in kind."

"Since when do you not give a man the right to a trial for his crimes, Cully? Or are your angel wings gettin' a little blackened while you slum it with all us lowlifes?"

"Ain't no slummin' on my part, Louis. They would have been given a chance had they not come in with their guns drawn and killin' on their minds," Cully said as Shorty pulled himself off of the floor. "Every time you rob the railway, you put innocent lives in danger, and I can't take any chances."

"So what now?"

"Now, you're gonna stand on that side of the room, and I'll stand over here. It's just the two of us. You can say what you need to get off your chest, and then I'm gonna make you an offer." Cully moved into position.

"This some kind of trick?"

"Ain't got no cards up my sleeve or nothin'. This is just a chat between two misunderstood individuals." Cully took his hat off and placed it on a table near the bedroom door.

"Fine, I'll bite," Shorty agreed. "You nearly killed me last time we met, remember? I was runnin' with that other gang with only a few robberies under my belt. I hated you for not givin' me the same offer you gave everybody else."

"Here's your chance." Cully raised his arms out to the side.

Chapter 14

Charlotte woke up to the smell of Wolf's hair oils and gunpowder. Tears burned in her eyes as she slumped against his strong chest. She had never felt so safe in her entire life. Just his presence was proof that she had not fantasized her rescue. Cully and the others had come for her.

She didn't recognize the man who rode on the other horse, but she spotted Bull's wiggling form as he tried to roll off the saddle he was strapped to. Wolf used his fingers to lift Charlotte's chin, forcing her to meet his gaze. The knife wound in her side burned like red fire, but she tried to hide her pain.

Wolf arched one of his unruly brows. "I know you better than that, Charlotte Dean. Don't you hide from me," he said. Each syllable was gently colored by his accent although his words were crisp and clear. "You hurt?"

She shook her head. "I'll live, Wolf. But you came back for me, thank you. I knew you wouldn't leave me behind."

"There was no way I was going to leave you to be tortured by those animals again. It was horrible not knowing what had happened to you." The pad of Wolf's calloused thumb stroked her cheek as he spoke. "But you're safe now, Charlotte."

Charlotte curled herself up against his warmth. Strangers stared, but she couldn't care less. She knew it was indecent for a woman to be so forward with a man—especially a white woman and a native. But Wolf had become her protector over the years, her damaged warrior who fought at her back no matter what.

Charlotte ran her fingers through the long, raven-colored locks of hair that fell over his shoulders. It distracted her from the pain and made her feel like everything had been set right. Her other hand touched a new scar on his chin that hadn't been there when she had been taken by Shorty and his gang.

He flinched at her touch but didn't move away. Wolf's skin was smooth and tan, evidence of the long hours they had spent in the sun while they had worked together a few months back. His eyes were the shade of exotic chocolates, framed by impossibly long lashes. Charlotte would never forget the way he had looked at her the day they met. Like she had been an angel who fell from grace.

After that day, it had only felt normal to stick together. Eventually the others had joined their little family. Charlotte closed her eyes and tried to shut out the memory of Jake, Midnight, Leo, and Isaac. Good men had died over what? Greed? No, it was worse. Charlotte knew that Shorty had robbed those trains out of boredom not necessity. If it had been about need, the robberies would have ended long ago.

Wolf's hands rubbed calming circles against her back. She allowed him to comfort her even when she knew he was the one who needed to be comforted the most. He had lost his cousin and best friend while trying to defend the people on the train. Charlotte blamed herself. She had suggested the contract.

"Don't you even think about it, Charlotte?"

She was caught off guard by the forcefulness of his words.

"I know you're feeling guilty about everything that happened. Like I said, I know you too well. I've blamed myself enough for the both of us," he said. "All we do now is put this to rest, and then we move on from it."

Charlotte didn't contradict him; she was too weak to argue. The pain eased into a dull sting, but she couldn't feel her fingers.

When they arrived in Aspen, the man who rode with them helped her off the horse. His eyes bulged. "Wolf…" he croaked.

Wolf looked down, so Charlotte followed his gaze. He was covered in blood. Her blood. It even trickled down the side of the saddle. The man who held her started off to find a doctor.

"Is she going to make it, my friend?" Wolf's voice cracked as he choked back his tears.

"I do not know. I am not even sure a doctor will agree to help," Mateo said before saying something in Spanish. "An Indian and a Mexican riding into town with an injured white woman does not look good, amigo."

They helped her inside the doctor's office, aware of the crowd that had amassed, but chose to disregard the sneers. Wolf called out, "We need help!"

There was no response for several minutes. Impatient, Wolf wandered through the small rooms of the building in search of anyone who could help. Several of the staff looked at him with disgust, so he grabbed supplies and hurried back to Charlotte. "Mateo, do you know how to mend a stab wound?"

"I've seen my sister Maria work magic, but Charlotte has lost a lot of blood. I'm not sure she will make it through the surgery," Mateo answered grimly between clenched teeth.

"You've killed dozens, if not hundreds of people durin' your raids. I'm sure you believe all of your actions are justified by your own reasonin', but you'll have to face the consequences for your crimes one way or another," Cully said. He risked a step forward, but Shorty was so focused on his anger that he didn't notice.

"Why can't I be wealthy, too? Why should the railroad companies have all the money? The railroad companies are tearin' this world apart just to get from one place to the next just a little faster," Shorty fumed. "What will happen to the men like us when there ain't anymore mountains or forests left?"

Cully had often wondered the same thing.

Shorty slowly loaded the revolver in his hand before returning it to the holster on his hip. "You need men like me Cully. Without us, there ain't no use for you."

"When the time comes for me to retire, I'll do it with the knowledge that I didn't stop fightin' until every last one of your kind was either behind bars or planted beneath the daisies." He placed the revolver he carried into the holster. "Money is not an excuse for murder. I know you like to think that you and I are alike in some ways, but all the men that have claimed to be like me in the past have fallen short."

"If money ain't a reason for murder, then what is? You think the railroad company ain't killed nobody? What about all the workers caught in the explosions or the ones that starve or get beaten to death? And it's all to line their pockets."

Cully shook his head. "Ain't no company I've ever come across that hadn't built themselves up by beatin' somebody else down. But you're stealin' these same workers' payroll, Shorty. So you ain't no man of the people."

"Seems like you and I are at a stalemate, then."

"That can be easily amended." Cully felt the cold wind blow in through the window and calm the burning flush against his cheeks. The pain in his arm was near unbearable—it was likely that the bullet had fractured something. "I'm gonna give you the opportunity to turn yourself in. Only this one opportunity, no more excuses."

"What's the other option?" Shorty asked.

"Quick draw," Cully stated with confidence.

He watched as Shorty slid his poker face down like a mask. The outlaw must not have been a very skilled shooter if he was that nervous. No wonder he had never been the first outlaw on the train during the raids.

"You wanted the chance I gave everybody else. So turn yourself over to me and go to trial for your crimes, or we draw fire now and one of us ain't walkin' away from this dance."

Shorty laughed in disgust. He reached for his gun, but it never left the holster. Cully outdrew him and fired all three bullets from the cylinder.

The outlaw slumped to his knees before he fell to the floor. His blood mingled with Charlotte's on the once pristine wood. Cully groaned deep in his chest and walked over and lifted the body of Louis "Shorty" Gerhard over the shoulder opposite of his injured arm. His muscles protested against the weight.

He carried the body over to the horse Shorty had originally escaped on. Cully strapped the legendary train robber to his mount and led the horse over to Samson. It took nearly all of his strength, but Cully was able to pull himself up and into the saddle. "Let's head to town, Samson."

The unpredictable weather of Independence Pass fortunately had turned neutral for once. No snow, rain, hail, or even bone-chilling temperatures kept Cully from reaching Aspen in less than two hours. He pulled the horses over to the sheriff's office and tied them to the hitching post—but not before he nearly fell off of Samson in a graceless attempt to dismount.

He stumbled when trying to enter through the doorway, but the heaviness in his body was suddenly relieved. Cully looked over at the man who supported his weight. Mateo smirked at him and gave him a look that said Cully would definitely owe them all a round of drinks for the extra trouble he put them through.

"How's Charlotte?" Cully mumbled.

"I was able to do what I could, but I am no miracle worker like Maria. It took until she nearly died for a nurse to decide to help us. Wolf is with her now."

"And how is he doin' after all of this?"

"Not well. I think after losing his cousin, he would not be able to go on if he lost Charlotte as well. He is a strong man, but there are certain things that can make a strong man weak," Mateo said with a wisdom that had not always been there.

Or maybe it had, and Cully just never noticed before.

Mateo helped him in to meet the sheriff.

Chapter 15

"The body of Louis "Shorty" Gerhard is out there on the back of one of those horses. His pal, Maurice "Bull" Burton is outside over at the doctor's office," Cully grunted out. "I'm sure with a little persuasion, he will be interested in spillin' his guts under the threat of goin' to trial. Seein' as he's the only one in the gang left alive who can take on the charges for the crimes, he's more than aware of what is at stake."

The sheriff jumped to action, running outside to confirm Cully's announcement. Shock and disbelief registered on the man's face. Cully didn't know if he was offended by that expression or not. But in the meantime, he needed to get the bullet out of his arm before he got lead poisoning—or with his luck, something worse.

Mateo assisted him in the long walk to the doctor's office. Cully told the sheriff to send a telegram to William S. Jackson in Denver and to come find him if he had any questions.

A woman scrubbed blood off of the floor as they walked in. The amount of red staining the area made Cully's heart clench. Miss Dean didn't deserve what happened to her. Even if she rode that gray area like so many others, Cully had the feeling that she might just be one of the good guys. Sure, he had his doubts in the beginning, but she had risked her life more than once to save him and the others.

Mateo tossed him into a chair and went to get the doctor who had agreed to help them. He was already covered in so much blood, Cully wanted to be anywhere else in time than that moment. Mateo said, "You should have seen how much was on Wolf when I lowered Charlotte off of his lap."

There wasn't much hope that she would recover, but hope and faith were two different things in his world. So Cully did something he hadn't done in years: he said a prayer for Charlotte to make it through these hard times.

After the local doctor did what he could for Charlotte, cleaning her up and applying a bandage, they all boarded the next train back to Denver. The doctor had sent a telegraph to the Denver General Hospital who were expecting their incoming patient.

———————

A week later, Cully stood in William S. Jackson's office for what felt like the hundredth time since he had accepted the initial contract. The polished man across the desk beamed with gratitude. He had even attempted to hug Cully at some point, but Cully wasn't too fond of hugging people he didn't consider family. He settled for a handshake.

"Thank you," the man said. "No words can describe how grateful I am. You get everything promised in your original contract, and the sheriff will throw in the reward money for the other outlaws you took care of in the process."

The sheriff broke in then. "Because of you, six wanted men were brought to justice. Maurice "Bull" Burton told us where all the money had been hidden in the cabin at Independence Pass. He even handed over whatever information he could think of to lessen his charges. We have everything we need to keep these things from happening again to the Denver & Rio Grande Western Railroad."

Cully sighed because he knew what came next. It wasn't that he didn't feel proud or grateful, it was just that he didn't want another plaque or ribbon to clutter the shelves in his home. Nevertheless, he accepted the honors and whatever else came with it. He even bit his tongue and sat through the many photographs they insisted he pose for.

Thankfully, he wasn't taken before a crowd in the grimy state he was in. After nearly a month of nothing but campfire gruel, subpar food from the inns, and no bath, Cully was ready to start gnawing at his belt if he didn't get a home-cooked meal. Heck, the belt probably had more sustenance than anything else he had eaten on the road.

Even when they rode on the trains that hadn't been attacked, Cully never ate the meal they offered when the others did. He usually gave his meal to whatever passenger hadn't been able to afford his or her own.

Cully kept his smile in place until he walked out of the company's building. He met up with Wolf and Mateo a few minutes later and handed them their share. Mateo hugged him carefully, mindful of his injuries. Wolf shook his hand. Cully walked with them to the hospital in Denver where Charlotte had been recovering.

He used some of his own money to pay for her medical treatment, waving off the protests from Wolf who had offered. When the bickering was finally over, he was escorted to Charlotte's room.

She was still pale, and she could barely move, but she was still alive—and that was all that mattered. He sat beside her on the bed. A smile slid across her face when she looked up at him.

"Hear you killed Shorty," Charlotte said in a raspy voice. "Would have loved to have been the one to take him down. But thank you. I know it had to have been hard letting him get away the first time, but it wasn't your fault."

"I put all of that behind me when I realized what was really important that we were fightin' for—and that was you," he stated. "Gettin' you back and takin' down the gang became our only priority, Charlotte. I did it mostly to repay you even if I hadn't known it at the time. Revenge ain't what I'm all about."

Charlotte Dean was grateful when Cully and Mateo left her alone to speak with Wolf in private. There was so much he needed to know and so much she wanted to tell him before it was too late and he walked away. "I know I've been difficult."

"I would not have used those words to describe you." Wolf winked at her playfully, eager to distract her thoughts. She shoved him as best as she could in her weakened state. He grabbed her hand and placed a kiss on her knuckles.

"Do you know what you are to me, Wolf?"

He thought for a moment. "I am your protector and your friend, Charlotte."

Charlotte knew Wolf hated to see her cry, but she didn't care. She wanted to cry—she deserved to cry and know that she wouldn't be mocked for it. "I love you, Wolf. I always have."

"Then why did you flirt with Jake so often... or even Cully the night we met him? It hurts to see you so casual with other men, Charlotte. I've loved you since the day we first met."

"I didn't think you had looked at me that way," she admitted. "You were so playful and wild, unwilling to let anything tame you or settle you down in any way. I didn't want you tame, Wolf. I wanted that playful and wild side that you showed everybody else. We bantered and joked, but you kept me away and treated me differently."

"Nothing good could come from us being together."

"Why? Because of the color of my skin?" Charlotte asked furiously. "I don't care about that. All I see is good in our future. I see happiness and a family with you. Nothing else matters but us, Wolf. Don't think about what anyone else thinks."

Cully was annoyed that Charlotte insisted on leaving Denver less than two weeks after getting injured. He paced up and down the street, waiting for Wolf to help her out. Cully had offered to buy them passage on a stagecoach, but he got turned down with a single glare. He really hated his inability to disrespect or even disagree with most women. His life would be a lot easier if he just knew how to talk to them.

Mateo snickered as he leaned up against the side of his horse, a hat pulled low over his brow. Cully finally caught sight of them. He ran over and took Charlotte from Wolf's arms so that he could mount the horse. Cully then passed her back to Wolf, but not before Charlotte placed a kiss on his cheek that made Wolf growl at him... like an actual growl.

Charlotte cackled with unbridled laughter before holding her side. Wolf nuzzled against her hair like a possessive beast trying to mark his mate with his scent. Cully thought it was a bit strange, but he didn't say anything. Mateo, however — "I can hear the wedding bells already, amigos! Now, go! Off into the wilderness and build your new life. Have a few puppies and don't forget to invite me for the holidays!"

Cully whapped Mateo on his back so hard he started coughing.

"That was not so nice, señor."

It was Cully's turn to laugh, finding it impossible to ignore Mateo's charm and humor. "What's next?" he asked.

"I go find Maria, and you take that time off you wanted."

The End

Could I get you to consider leaving a review on Amazon? It would be appreciated.

More westerns are in the works. Meanwhile, visit my Amazon Author Page for a complete list of previous titles.